Snitch

Orion Pharoah

Published by Subconscious Literature, 2022.

SNITCH

First edition. April 23, 2022.

Copyright © 2022 Orion Pharoah.

ISBN: 979-8986124513

Written by Orion Pharoah.

A Special Thank you!

As a writer, it's only my imagination that goes into the manufacturing of a story; but it takes a village to produce a manuscript worthy of publishing. I would like to take the time to say thank you to my beautiful wife for all of her love and support. I want to acknowledge the love, patience and understanding of my family, brothers, and friends as I've ventured down the rabbit's hole to turn Snitch into a living ideal! Thank you all for your love and support. ***Pops, I miss you.*** *Orion Pharoah*

Snitch

By: Orion Pharoah

Chapter 1

The paddle of the canoe gently danced on the crystal blue Bora Bora water, as it floated towards Pauline. She sat in front of a brilliantly lit vanity looking out the window. Two beautiful Polynesian women were assisting her, making sure her makeup and hair were exactly right for the big day, as the water drifted slowly under her feet. She looked down and saw a parade of tropical fish dancing under the glass bottom of her Honeymoon Suite. She gazed astonishingly at the stranger in the mirror- she only recognized herself by the sparkling hazel eyes holding back tears as the ladies gently braided a crown of tropical flowers into her hair. She stood in amazement, waving her hands across her eyes trying to hold back the tears. The canoe gently docked at her suite which sat on the end cap of the row in a crystal blue lagoon with a magnificent grass covered volcano as her backdrop.

A young warrior greeted her by placing palm leaves on the wet sand just beyond the surf and grabbing her hand as she stepped out of the canoe. The dazzling Bora Bora sand felt like white roses between her toes caressing her feet. Her second step caused tears to glisten down her cheeks allowing her beautiful hazel eyes to out sparkle the waters of the South Pacific Sea. Her husband- to-be waiting with all smiles less than 30 yards away in pure astonishment. Seeing her for the first time, he was captivated by the floor-length, ice white satin of the fitted trumpet, with white lace, and spaghetti strap style dress. The back of the wide-open bodice revealing Pauline's beautiful cinnamon skin as the train gently caressed the sand. Her waiting bridegroom stood proud with the tribal chief, admiring his breath-taking bride-to-be. As she took her third step onto the soft sand, her soul took a peek behind the curtain allowing her to breathe in her new life. She beamed. It had been an adulthood of mistakes and misguided decisions that two little words were finally going to erase and give her the future she once believed was only a dream. Pauline's breath hitched as her pupils dilated, blacking out their once captivating hazel glow. She began her next step and the whites of her perfectly manicured French tips began to pierce her palms, crushing her bouquet of Tahitian gardenia she was holding. The only clue to the sudden halt of her bridal march was a crisp whistle through the air, leaving a slight pop in the sand. Pauline's toes curled deep into the beach as the massive lacerations and torn veins in her neck began to send distress signals to her heart, causing it to pump three times the amount of blood through her body. The projectile removed the majority of her esophagus eliminating her ability to speak. As the unregulated flow of blood spilled over into her lungs, Pauline reached to her groom. The arterial spray peppered her dress and the sand, providing an alarm to all in attendance as strokes of crimson painted the paradise. Pauline, in one last attempt to speak, expelled a large gulp of blood onto the sand, the ominous sign that her lungs had been saturated with fluid.

The wedding party began to tumble over each other as the Polynesian ceremony King tackled the agonizing bridegroom to the wooden deck. He lay there reaching for Pauline crying out as her lifeless body hit the sand. The sniper's bullet had successfully found its target.

Chapter 2

Assistant Director Samuel Jeffries of the FBI stood in his office with his third cup of coffee reviewing Pauline's case file and the ballistics report from Bora Bora. Samuel escorted his team into the huddle room - he worked with the best. Senior Agent Kevin Goodson, a 7-year veteran and former counterintelligence operative with a focus on Russian military; Special Agents Sarah Montgomery and Charles Stevens, two ex-navy SEALs, and the newest member to the team, Special Agent Cynthia Prince.

Pictures of Pauline's autopsied body were up on the huddle room's huge smart board screen sparking Sarah immediately,

"Oh my God, isn't that our star witness from the Fregoso case?"

Charles chimed in, "She's definitely seen better days."

"Good thing the old man died in prison." She replied.

Samuel never looked up from the case file, instead he struggled to keep his emotions in check realizing that Pandora's Box was open. He focused with the understanding that his team had now unwittingly stepped into a manhunt that would force them to navigate the razor's edge.-a thin, sharp line between political power and international conflict. This killer brought back the rage within himself, a hauntingly familiar sickness the Fregoso case created as he prepared to tell the story between the lines that didn't exist in the FBI's report.

He took a breath and focused his team, "Pauline was going to be the first material witness ever on record to testify against Frank Fregoso." Samuel paused as he watched Cynthia scribbling down notes. He always gave her time to complete her dictation. Special Agent Prince was the FBI's best forecaster. Her attention to detail and ability to use those observations to make leaps into investigations that otherwise were cold, earned her a spot at the table. Samuel focused on Cynthia, "I know you've dissected the case files, but this case is going to require a full history lesson. The old man was the only reason witness protection had to create Pauline Lucy. She was once a mid-level money launderer working under cover with false credentials in a bank in Panama. She was literally a gift in forming a case against the once elusive Frank Fregoso.

Chapter 3

(Exactly two years and eighteen days ago)
Only 7 doors down the hallway from the team huddle room a phone rings at
Director Jason Murphy's office.

"Murphy." He paused as he heard all the information given on the other-side of the line, "On American soil!? Absolutely Sir. I'll send Samuel and his team now."

Murphy rushed down the hall into Assistant Director Samuel Jeffries' office,

"Samuel, he's on American soil!"

"Who?"

"Number one," Murphy smiled.

Samuel jumped up from his desk. "Frank?"

Director Murphy handed him the intel advising, "Wheels up in 20 minutes."

Samuel briefed his team in route to LAX.

"Ladies and gentlemen Frank Fregoso is confirmed to be at a medical office outside Los Angeles, that's all we have. We need to be clear that we all understand no intelligence means anyone in the medical center could be there to protect Frank."

Senior agent Goodson spoke up, "Hold on, Frank Fregoso is the sole controlling hand of war and battle strategies for the better part of half a century. His organization is believed to damn near decide who wins or loses in the world and we are running blind into an unsecured building for an 89-year-old man with 50 years of people owing him favors?"

Samuel smiled, "Absolutely, we will get to the front door of the office with no weapons drawn and prepare to breach."

Sarah, smiling at Charles questioned, "Who hates us?" The two former Navy SEALs always had confidence in every mission.

Charles addressed the team, "Let's think this through. Frank has been king for a long time but this is a man who plays chess with presidents. Fifty years of power across every country has him on a stop and interrogate list that has never been enforced by anyone. Hell, we don't even have a front facing photo of this man. He has more power than any of us could ever fathom but like Goodson said, he's 89 years old. There hasn't been a war or any type of major conflict in a while, and I think Frank's organization is on autopilot. He is at a private multimillion-dollar oncology facility- he's sick. He's not traveling with an entourage, he's been King for 50 years. Who's going to challenge him?"

"Guys, Charles is right." Samuel confirmed. "We're going in. This is Frank Fregoso. If he talks - gives us anything, we will be able to bring down the violence and corruption that is decimating our country. We have enough Intel to know that Frank's there. Ladies and gentlemen that's all we need."

Chapter 4

Frank Fregoso sat down with an old friend and specialists, "Today I want you to talk to me as a friend, don't take pity on this old ma; I've had a life that only Emperors and Pharaohs would comprehend. Show me one last loyalty," He smiled, looking at him.

Dr. Shelli Bukhara looked across his desk at a man who for fifteen years had become more than a patient. Frank was truly his friend, there for him and his family during horrible times in Pakistan and celebrating monumental victories with his new life in America. He grabbed both of Frank's hands squeezed them tight then released them taking a deep breath, "Frank you're dying and there are only two options. The first, walk out of here and do nothing. Frank, if you make that choice there's no guarantee that tonight won't be your last night on this planet, and you'll go to bed with that storm cloud over you for the next six months, but the storm will catch you, I just don't know when. There's a good chance that some night between tonight and no more than six months from tonight," He paused. "Frank, you'll never wake up again." Holding back tears before giving his second option, he continued, "Or you can fight it, give yourself a solid 9 to 10 months."

"What kind of fight is that?" Frank inquired.

"A fight in which eight of those months you'd be in more pain and misery than I care to explain to a friend, but you would be alive, Frank."

"Your loyalty means more to me than your diagnosis." Frank said, looking down at his phone. He stood up, "Let's walk to the back one last time and destroy my files."

The two men stood at the incinerator loading files, CDs, and flash drives and as the doctor closed the door, Frank threw his phone in with all the medical documents.

"My friend you have been given a final payment that is enough to ensure that you, nor your next generation will never have to give this kind of news again. But I know that your heart will allow you to keep helping others. Obrigado."

Frank hugged him then turned to walk out the office. Outside in the foyer Samuel stood with his team nervously waiting to see a man that had reigned from the shadows. Frank smiled as he stepped confidently into the foyer.

He addressed him, "Assistant Director Samuel Jeffries, eying you and your gifted team here tells this old man not all of my close friends have remained loyal."

Kevin's first thought as he saw the man they have referred to for years as the king of war, was so powerful it became audible, "Holy shit, that's Frank Fregoso and he knows who we are."

Frank begin to speak again, "You and your team may remain calm there will be no fight, I will go with you to your SUV's. I didn't have a ride home anyway."

Frank stuck his wrist out towards Jeffries and Samuel looked him in the eyes, "That won't be necessary, Mr. Fregoso."

"Please call me Frank." He smiled.

Samuel repeated, "That won't be necessary Frank, please come with us."

The team drove urgently to the LAX hanger, three SUV's deep: Sarah and Samuel accompanying Frank with Kevin driving lead and Charles running flank. They loaded the waiting G6 and flew to Denver International Airport with their cooperative, yet completely silent detainee. They hit the tarmac and loaded the waiting SUV that was being secured by three fully armed rotating helicopter units, running ghost reconnaissance during the transportation to the FBI interrogation center. Frank smiled looking out of the window and finally broke his silence, "I take it anything I care to say will be used to keep me on American soil and as long as possible?"

Samuel replied, "The American justice system is all ears, Frank."

Frank cut a small grin and as the team turned their heads to look at him,

"I find it very fascinating that of all the commodities in the world, information seems to cost the absolute most." As they pulled into the facility Frank continued,

"Assistant Director Samuel Jeffries, I imagine you will get a plaque on the wall for this, and your team will be honored. You are an exceptionally good agent Assistant Director, but if you care to entertain an old man, just know not all sources of information, witnesses, and smiling faces are loyal good people. Sometimes loyalty shows its face in places you don't understand. I wish you good fortune in your career Assistant Director Samuel Jeffries."

Samuel and the team were rendered speechless with a mix of emotions as they sat in awe at the underground entrance.

They were all brought back to attention when Frank looked out the window at the beautiful tree line and said,

"I believe you and the CIA have good intentions. It's time." As the guards made their way to the SUV.

Frank Fregoso was led into the facility in Boulder, Co and directly into the first-floor conference room. Section Chief Kase Richardson walked in, shook Frank's hand and addressed him, "Mr. Fregoso, I will ask your patience as we process your paperwork to determine the best course of action for your stay. Frank smiled and nodded and Kase excused himself. He returned 45 minutes later with a somber, steady voice and advised Frank that his stay there would be as a guest of the CIA. The section chief stated, "Mr. Fregoso, you will have embassy calls daily, beginning tomorrow. At this time, Sir, is there anything that the CIA can do to make your stay as suitable as possible?"

Frank rose his head slightly to look out of the conference room, " I imagine that local state facilities must have security lighting only in the late evenings. Would it be possible to have a room that utilizes the natural moonlight more than others, so that I may play chess at the same time I would when I was home?"

Kase forced a smile and answered, "I'm sure we can get you a suite on the top floor, Mr. Fregoso, just steady as we make accommodations."

He thanked the section chief and that evening, Frank checked in. He was a model houseguest for three months. One phone call every day and outside of the first conversation in the conference room, he never said a word. Until one evening Frank spoke on his daily call, only two words that have never been translated, and that night Frank met his end, shortly after the guard's rotation. He died from a single shot to the heart with a hand loaded, custom made AX50 sniper round. His embassy was notified and they were at the doorsteps of the facility within an hour. The only thing the CIA was able to place were five tracking devices. None of them ever left Colorado. They were found in a private hangar along with the coffin provided, at Denver International Airport.

Chapter 5

Samuel wrestled with a gut-wrenching guilt building in his soul as he thought about how Frank met his end. His facial anguish was enough to grab the teams concern as he reached slowly to his laptop to change the picture of Pauline to the sniper round collected in Bora Bora. He allowed the team a moment to collect themselves as the spent AX50 round sat triumphantly on the screen. They sat collectively in silent shock, looking at the exact same sniper ammunition that had haunted them for two years, extracted from Frank Fregoso's chest. Cynthia broke the silence, "Team, these shots are two years apart so that means we've got an active shooter, the bonus this time around is we have a witness in custody, scared to death of the new regime and the tactics used to complete the coup." She paused a moment to gauge everyone's face and when she could read that they were moving past their disappointment, she continued, "Eli is cooperating against

Brussia and once we let him know about Pauline, he'll give us this gun for hire."

The team, realizing the Fregoso case was now active again, collected themselves and Samuel addressed them, "Let's figure out what cases we still have open that's not Frank related and get it passed off or closed. If there is someone you love that is used to seeing your beautiful faces, I suggest you text them a heartfelt apology."

Kevin walked to the whiteboard and taped down the most recent photographs of the seven-man- pyramid that formed the world's most powerful organization known by the FBI. Standing back looking at the photos he addressed his team, "Let's start at the top. The picture that we're looking at of Frank Fregoso was taken while detained in Colorado. What we have discovered since that photo-with the help of the NSA and CIA, is that Frank came into power more than 50 years ago. How remains unknown, but Frank did not want the spotlight, his organization had never made any moves towards any type of visible power. Instead, Frank has kept to the shadows keeping secret alliances around the globe. According to our friends at the CIA there's no modernized battle technology that Frank Fregoso's organization didn't have a hand in creating or own the majority of the manufactured product. This makes the Fregoso organization massive enough to carry the title number one arms distributor to the world from C4 detonation to satellite-controlled reconnaissance missions. Somewhere up the line that technology came from Fregoso over the last 50 years, so as much as we have discovered these past few years, we actually don't have many details about the organization. What we didn't know for fifty years, was who where these seven men or their major functions. How things move or information on the manufacturing, research, and facilities. Who's working with him? Who's not working with him? These are all questions no agency has been able to ascertain. Frank Fregoso spent a lifetime ahead of the US, Russian, and British intelligence. He really was King and his round table is comprised of the best the underworld has known."

Kevin paced back and forth as he broke it all down, "Reporting directly to Frank are two of the most powerful men in the world: Vero Brussia, Russian American - if Frank's organization is truly running all things that are war, Brussia is his weapon of mass destruction. He ensures all deliveries and payments are made and has no hesitation in killing anyone that attempts to delay his operations. To his left, Aiden Gina, said to be of Spanish descent and was once going to be considered a top candidate as president of Spain. He is the polar opposite of Brussia. A political genius with a horrible narcissistic demeanor.

His temper may have got the best of him almost five years back because it is speculated that he killed an Interpol official. This put Gina on every peace-loving country's shit list, and like a damn Grand Master, Frank used the accusations to move his Bishop into exile; this allowed him to check-mate the organizations enemies from the shadows. This strategy from the limelight increased Gina's political power while making it more likely to find the Loch ness monster before locating Gina; but since hiding him, the Fregoso organization has gained some strong allies across South America. No one knows where he is for sure, but he does show up from time to time. Vero Brussia has two direct reports, both rowdy enough to earn his respect: Mickell Vosh and Eli Eugene. Vosh is one of the deadliest men in Russia, he runs all the Russian underground after a bloody upheaval. Eli operated right here under our nose in the United States, his work is ugly- he's a dirty player but has an inflated sense of loyalty to Frank. This loyalty and self-preservation sent him running to us."

Sarah picked up, "Eli has speculated that Brussia- at minimum, found the sniper that killed Fregoso, but muscle doesn't keep the empire healthy. The brain of the organization definitely runs through Gina's camp with Martin Groshki and Lorenzo Aldridge. Martin is a hand grenade in a ten-thousand-dollar suit; a forked-tongued- bully with no fear. With Gina in the wind, Martin has been running ground operations for the organization. He has insured not an ounce of power has been lost with Gina unable to perform face-to-face meetings. We have surveillance of him making frequent visits to different embassies and we imagine that's to ensure that cooperation is being kept. He's very well connected and his proclivity for ordering hits, has no boundaries, regardless of your level of influence." Sarah paused straining to fight back the sickening feeling the next member of the organization brought to surface. She lifted her hand to her face to manually remove the wrinkles he causes in her forehead, "Mr. Lorenzo Aldridge, aka Carl Stephanie, was the money of the Fregoso organization. He was Frank's chief accountant and Aden Gina's right hand. Three years ago he slid into Washington and on FBI doorsteps like a gift, except he didn't want to talk about Frank; he had information that was going to make it really hard to incarcerate him. A joint task force consisting of Britain, the US, and Russia had been working to eliminate some very violent men from Russia's barbaric past and Aldridge had all the key information to flushing them out of hiding. I'm talking every piece of information needed to completely dismantle the Russian mob. Said he came to us because he was scared that Brussia would come after him. Once we agreed to keep him protected, he sang like a bird. We changed his identity and created Carl Stephanie and hid him faraway. Never has there been a more successful flip, the entire Russian Mafia took a hit that they would never recover from and after nine months of him testifying. He gladly faded away into witness protection, three months later Frank Fregoso was killed and Carl Stephanie disappeared. His girlfriend woke up in the middle of the night and he was gone but didn't take a thing."

Sarah stopped adjusting her beautiful, twisting, brunette curls out of her face and continued. "His disappearance brought Gina out of hiding long enough to get current pictures at a bank in Panama. 2.5

billion dollars were missing from the Fregoso organization and the last known offshore account it was bounced to, belongs to Carl Stephanie. We realized after the trace that we had been played."

Kevin broke in saying, "Lorenzo and the money disappeared simultaneously with the reemergence of Russian under-ground. It seemed as Mickell had breathed life back into the mob. He brought in an army of men and set up shop in the bones of the Russian mafia we helped eliminate. Seems somehow through Frank's death and Lorenzo's testimony, Vero Brussia had taken over the entire northern hemisphere."

***

Deputy Director John Tanner sat perfectly upright at his desk. His suit showed no sign of wear. Seven decades of life showed in the wrinkles of his face. Retired CIA Section Chief now one of the FBI's greatest assets on international terrorism. He put on his suit jacket as the wrinkles in his face turned his stoic face into a wise smile, causing his sleek silver hair to rise slightly as his hand reached down to grab the manila folder on his desk. He walked leisurely down the hallway to the huddle room door. The team looked up as he swung the door open and Samuel addressed him, "Can I help you Tanner?"

Tanner took his time to make eye contact with the entire team leading his way up to Samuel as he spoke, "As of 9:45 AM, your entire team is considered vital in a national security risk. It's been deemed that anyone working or have worked any case connected to Frank Fregoso are prioritized section 17. This means until the Fregoso case is put to rest the NSA will be paying close attention to all of you."

Samuel, focused on the manila folder under John's arm asked, "Why have we been put on alert?"

Deputy Director Tanner handed the folder to Samuel exclaiming, "Eli Eugene was found dead this morning and two FBI agents hospitalized upon his retrieval."

Kevin bolted to his feet and Charles put his hand on his shoulder. He asked, "Boss is this true?"

Samuel opened the file looking down as the lines in his forehead began to crease and he squeezed the bridge of his nose as Tanner walked out, slamming the door.

Chapter 6

Samuel watched Deputy Director Tanner exit the huddle room as his thoughts jumped to Frank Fregoso. He cleared his throat, "This is Vero Brussia telling us that he owns an incredibly talented killer. The level of disrespect to the American justice system that these acts boast is unfathomable."

Sarah asked, "Are we sure that it's just Brussia? This could be how the Fregoso organization is going to run from now on."

Kevin removed his glasses, "Brussia's team made the power play for the northern hemisphere and Eli was a team captain. He possessed all the information we would have needed to bring down everything Brussia built. Couple that with Gina knee deep in an Interpol investigation. There's no way in hell Gina risks the wrath that killing two FBI witnesses in less than three days is going to bring."

Charles pounded the table, "I agree with Goodson. This is bold, this isn't politically correct. Gina would find this distasteful, but how do we know it's the same hired gun?"

Cynthia thought about it, "We know it's the same because of the level of intelligence. It is not the weapon so much as it is that it takes the same mental edge. Finding and eliminating anyone protected by our agencies is not a skill we see often. His specialty is intelligence. There's not a lock he can't pick or a puzzle he can't solve. It's definitely him."

Samuel swallowed hard, "OK, then we know what we're listening for, these agents have talked to no one. They had been in a room waiting to be debriefed and they're being escorted in right now. We need every detail and we need them to step past the shock and tell us everything. If this assassin is a solo artist, he knows witness protection, FBI, and CIA protocol. Plus he is extremely patient and we don't have time to be. Vero Brussia is moving to take full power and he's doing it out in the open so let's pray his arrogance gives us a step ahead. We have two agents in Florida who possess information and the only way we're going to get it out of there shocked system is to lead them."

Making eye contact with every one of them as he talked, he continued,

"Team I know it's a lot to absorb but we will need to remain focused on information."

Cynthia chimed in, "We are going to have to assume that these agents could have been in on this, two federally protected witness's dead in less than 72 hours is not possible from the outside." Charles, in agreement piped up, "Then no information given, but let's get them on the line."

Samuel started the conversation once the men on the other line picked up. "Gentlemen, Assistant Director Samuel Jeffries here with my team. I want you to speak freely about today's events."

"Yes Sir." One agent spoke out.

Samuel addressed the speaker phone, "Gentlemen allow me to start by saying thank you for your service. I know what you've gone through today has challenged a lot of beliefs that you held dear but more than anything gentlemen- you're alive, and soon you'll be home with your families. Please do your best to relax, I want you to be incredibly detailed and walk me through your assignment from the very beginning."

A man's voice started speaking, "Thank you Sir, this is Agent Sorenson. I picked up agent Wesley at 07:00 hours, Tuesday morning."

Charles stopped him, "Why 7:00 o'clock on Tuesday? That's a full 24 hours before the incident."

"Yes sir," the voice confirmed, "We never know the priority level of our assignments until it's given, and Eli Eugene required an overnight isolation." Agent Wesley answered.

"Thank you, agent. Please proceed," said Charles.

Agent Sorenson continued, "I picked him up and we decided since this was a new assignment day, we would bypass breakfast and go directly into the office."

"Agents?" Senior agent Kevin Goodson asked, "is that typical routine?"

"Yes sir, "choice days" insures no permanent routine. Once we were given our assignment, Eli Eugene transfers to a secure location for debriefing. Our cell phones were collected, and we were given the full priority level of the asset. We were immediately greeted by our section supervisor and taken into special operations for retrieval protocols. Dinner with the command Sergeant and lights out at 21:00 hours then at 03:30 hours we were assigned cell phones and headed out, along with six decoy units given specific GPS direction. Agent Wesley and I arrived 5 minutes early in front of the asset's safe-house."

Cynthia asked, "Anything out of place or odd up to this point?"

"No ma'am." He replied. "it was perfect, but if I may? Perfect like picture perfect, like, strangely perfect."

"Okay, someone explain to me what I am not seeing." Samuel said frustrated.

Agent Sorenson begin to talk, "There was little traffic, it was a few cars, one or two tractor trailers and the flow was steady. Inside of the neighborhood there were three bikes spaced out between a few blocks and two joggers, one with headphones. The front of the house was textbook, from the morning paper to the spacing in the curtains and color coordination, showing there was absolutely no distress. Literally, the way I would write it in a training manual, Sir."

"Agent Wesley, do you confirm the same sense of too right?" Jeffries asked

"Yes Sir, nothing out of place, but looking back, it was laid out a little too nice."

"Thank you, agents please continue."

"Yes sir, with all positive signs confirmed we hit the garage door opener and pulled in beside Eli's car to perform the final interior check. The interior door to the mud room was propped open with the visible go bag on the floor which confirmed Eli was ready. We exited the car and came around through the mud room and immediately saw Eugenie Eli in the armchair with a very recent bullet wound to the head, Sir."

"Guys, Agent Montgomery here, define recent?"

Agent Sorenson cleared his throat, "Eli was sitting in the living room recliner with his head tilted back slightly looking at the door with a bullet hole directly through the skull. Eli's exit wound was still dripping onto the carpet."

"Alright, that is definitely recent. Please continue."

"That is as far as I go. Agent Wesley will have to continue." Sorensen stated as Agent Wesley took over the conversation.

"I heard a sharp whistle as I drew for my gun and Agent Sorensen hit the ground."

"Agent Wesley what happened next? Samuel asked.

"Sir, I woke up in the hospital."

"Agent Sorenson, what happened when you woke up?" He spoke up, "Sir I woke up 2 hours later on the mud room floor beside an unconscious Wesley and pulled a well-crafted tranquilizer out of my neck. I drew my weapon while simultaneously looking to see Wesley, with two projectiles in him. I called it in and searched the premises to find that Eli's body and car were gone and the garage door was open. We were taken to the hospital where it took adrenaline and two more hours for agent Wesley to gain consciousness and we have been here debriefing since our release."

Samuel took a deep breath running his fingers through his hair and lowered his tone saying, "Agent Sorenson, Agent Wesley, we thank you two gentlemen tremendously for your service. I want you to know that you have been given unconditional paid leave and I want to make sure that you are mentally and physically in the right place before you two brilliant agents get back in the saddle. Do you have any questions for me or my team?"

Agent Wesley asked, "how did they know things we learned less than 48 hours ago?"

"That's a particularly good question, Agent; I wish I had an answer for you. Right now, I want you to go home and be with your families and loved ones. Hug somebody you care about, Okay?" Samuel quickly responded.

"Thank you, Sir."

The conference room was silent for a moment as Samuel disconnected the line.

Keven stood up, "Brussia can't win like this! This is not how the law works! Who is this damn assassin and what's his motivation?"

Sarah chuckled at his emotional outburst.

"Apparently, somewhere between one and two-and-a half billion dollars. Like you said, you just don't become the owner of everything Russian underground for free."

Samuel with his head still in his hands looked up, "Brussia has orchestrated the murder of two federally protected witnesses, showing that he believes he is untouchable or extremely arrogant. Either way we are hella behind this hired gun and we will be in trouble if we don't catch up quick."

Charles chuckled nervously looking down at Cynthia's laptop, "It looks like we're in a storm of trouble boss, they just found Eli Eugene's body."

Pausing as Cynthia put it up on the screen, he continued,

"His car and body were found on the side of the road in opposite ditches. This photo is from the M.E.; it says official cause of death is a bullet wound to the head."

Samuel looked at the photo, "Cynthia, what does the medical report give as cause for opening up his throat during the autopsy?"

Referring to the line of stitches running vertical down Eli Eugene's throat.

"Sir, the medical examiner's report indicates that Eli was found face down with the stitches already in his neck. The incision was made postmortem, a section of his esophagus was removed and our "gun for hire" very intentionally stitched him back up."

Charles whispered to himself, "He was found face down in a ditch." He said loud, "Brussia is cleaning house and he just changed his assassin into a snitch killer with a very clear message to anyone willing to cooperate with us."

Samuel, looking from the screen back to his laptop's ballistics report said, "Since we don't have a name for this high-priced assassin, we're going to call him what he seems to despise. I think Snitch is a fitting name. Now that he's given us the same bullet two years apart, it's going to be his own bullet that locks him away for life. He must answer for Frank Fregoso's death and if he's counting on Brussia to have his back when the shit hits the fan, he should look back at his first assignment. We need to tie him to Eli's murder and find out who's helping him. Time to lose some sleep team, this Snitch character is seven steps ahead of us again and we have got to get caught up."

Chapter 7

Samuel sat in Director Murphy's office staring aimlessly out the window as the two of them searched desperately for words during their weekly one on one.

Murphy spoke up. "Samuel, fourteen months into the Fregoso assassination I made a personal decision to allow you to start focusing on being the great assistant director that you are. I made that decision because you were chasing a highly skilled assassin. A man so connected that no government agency had any inclination of his identity or origin. That decision made America a safer country by allowing you and your team to refocus. Samuel it's been two months and you're still chasing the same highly skilled, very well-connected assassin but unlike two years ago, we know exactly who orchestrated this. Vero Brussia and Mickell Vosh have taken over the Northern Hemisphere. This means Aiden Gina is either a trapped man, a dead man, or worse, a pissed man who was probably the rightful heir to the Fregoso throne. Samuel, Snitch is not going to miraculously manifest because of hard work or an intel leak- he's too smart. Understand it's Snitch that's smart, not his current employer. You don't take a job like Fregoso without understanding what it means to kill the King. Find a way to put cuffs on the organizer of this coup and he will be holding the leash of this beast. Your team needs to focus on Brussia, getting to him is your key to finding something on Snitch". He paused for a second.

"Samuel regarding your team, send them home to get a good night's rest and in the morning find these bastards. We will bring them to justice not only because Frank deserves it, but because they don't deserve to be monsters in a world that's trying to find a better path. There's not a day that I don't see your crew working, I know you're doing the best you can but they've been here all weekend into Monday morning. Let them get some rest, you'd be amazed what a fresh mind can spark." Director Murphy put his hand on Samuel's shoulder as he leaned against his desk.

"How Jason?" Samuel asked with his eye slightly glazed. "How am I supposed to rest? This feels different. Like I owe Frank more justice than dying in a cell at the behest of a maniac like Vero Brussia, and if I'm honest with myself, finding Snitch would at least prove that we didn't put him in a cage and set him up to die."

Murphy stopped him, "Samuel you and your team go home. Let yourself rest. In the morning we will route our course and if we decide we need to find Snitch, we will hunt him. Samuel when the King goes down there's a power struggle and right now, everybody's fighting for the top position and this thing is going to get ugly. Brussia just struck first with his secret weapon but all he did was strike first. Get some rest."

"You're right Jason." Samuel smiled, scratching his beard. "The team will appreciate a breather."

***

That evening in Manhattan, the majority of the workers at the International Tech building left for the day and the cleaning crew arrived to begin the process on the skyscraper. Snitch, in a three-piece Armani suit, overcoat and fedora, walked in with the hectic flow of traffic. He joined the elevator with the cleaning crew and stepped off on the 46th floor. He blended in seamlessly as the overtime crowd moved around excited to finally be going home. He found the corner office next to one of the firm's vice presidents and sat down to wait for the office building to empty.

Chapter 8

The Manhattan skyline changed from defining architecture to a sea of security lights and the stunning electrical bonanza that is Broadway Avenue, as Vice President Audrey Burkes worked diligently at her desk . Snitch stood up and removed his hat and coat then stepped out of the office gently walking next door into the only lit office, closing the door behind him.

She asked, "May I help you, Sir?"

Looking up when no response was given to see Snitch standing in front of her desk with his 10mm 1911 in his hand, the color left her face.

"No Audrey you can't help me; at this point in time you can't even help yourself." Snitch said as he walked around her desk closing her blinds.

"Audrey you helped steal money from Frank Fregoso and now you and your boyfriend are attempting to steal once again for the personal gain of Vero Brussia." He paused looking at the Authentic Katana on display on her bookshelf and holstered his weapon to slide it out of its sheath.

Audrey's voice trembled, "Please don't kill me! I was just doing what Joey asked me to. please." Tears running down her face, she broke down sobbing into her hands as Snitch walked over to a table next to her desk and pulled an item out of his pocket to replace the pawn on her custom chessboard. Putting the pawn in his pocket he stepped between Audrey and her desk placing his hand gently over her mouth and pressing the Katana against her rib cage. He began to whisper as her tears rippled over the fingers of his glove, "Audrey there are consequences for all acts against the King."

Audrey's body bucked slightly as the katana moved swiftly through her heart and out of the back of her Pride-More chair. There was a small whimper as Audrey's body went limp then he stepped away from the desk and closed the door behind him as he walked back to the corner office to wait for the 5AM rush of early risers and programmers coming into the Manhattan high rise so he could exit unnoticed. He walked two blocks and his car picked him up and pulled into the private parking at 157 W. 57th Street. Snitch exited the car with a box in hand and made his way quickly to a secure elevator, the penthouse doors opened softly and he walked past the spiral staircase into the kitchen and over to the island where he replaced the French press with a new one from the box. Satisfied with the new press, he sat down in front of the window in the living room to enjoy the New York sunrise over Central Park.

***

Sarah burst into the huddle room. "Guys, how about bagels and lox in Manhattan?"

"I'm always down for breakfast," Charles retorted, "but why?"

"Audrey Burkes!" Sarah exclaimed. "She is paying $16,000 a month for a swanky villa outside of Moscow."

"Who?" Kevin asked.

"Let me slow down." she smiled and took a breath.

"I woke up around 3 this morning, after a well dented 12 pack to a blaring news channel. The last thing I heard as I turned off the TV was how another bank was in trouble and I realized that Eli couldn't have been part of the original payment to Snitch, he hadn't turned to us yet. That means that there must be a new large payment so I went on the assumption that Brussia and our missing Carl would have to establish new banking lines outside of the Fregoso organization to ensure Gina remained clueless." She looked around to make sure everyone was all caught up and ran her hands through her short, brown hair as she continued, "I checked all foreign and domestic financial transfers and I uncovered a sixteen thousand-dollar insufficient funds transaction 72 hours ago on a property in Russia. A payment she has been making for over a year on a property dead center of the map on Kevin's top five tactical spots for Mickell Vosh."

The team jumped to their feet as Samuel told her "It's 6 am, tell us the rest on the way to New York, let's go!"

The team hurried out of the building to the airstrip.

Chapter 9

The New York sunrise peeked through the penthouse windows as Joey Malcom made his way downstairs to the kitchen. He hit the automatic shades and reached for his coffee press as the aroma of fresh ground beans filled the penthouse. He filled the coffee press and after a moment began to push down, holding the press firmly. Snitch sent a text activating a small explosive that ripped through the man's hands destroying the tissue to the bone and dispersing hot coffee across the kitchen. Malcom's back hit the dishwasher and he began to cry out Snitch walked into the dining area and addressed the distressed man.

"Lorenzo Aldridge." Snitch said confidently as Lorenzo's screams stopped with the realization that two identity changes and the FBI had not stopped the Fregoso family from finding him. He grabbed the towel beside him as he began to speak. "Those hands were once responsible for the growth and prosperity of the Fregoso organization-the same hands that betrayed his love and financed Frank Fregoso's death. Don't act like you honestly thought we wouldn't find out you became a snitch named Carl Stephanie for the FBI. You allowed the violence that is Vero Brussia and Mickell Vosh to form a huge storm cloud of anguish over Russia. When you were done using the Americans you were given enough money and Brussia protection to change everything about yourself but your disloyalty cannot be erased with multimillion-dollar plastic surgery. Lorenzo, you die today."

Unable to speak through his pain and sobbing, Lorenzo Aldridge could only tremble as Snitch pulled out the 1911 and twisted the silencer in position. Snitch smiled, "Joey, Carl, Lorenzo, I want you all to send a message no one can misinterpret."

The discovered man rested his head against the cabinet as Snitch pointed the gun to his face and cried out, "Please don't do this. Anything can be put right if you just let me live. I have money, just name your price." His plea was answered with two 10mm rounds to his face.

***

The blaring siren belting from the SUV traveling through lower Manhattan brought traffic to a halt at Liberty. Charles unbuckled and looked over Sarah's shoulder,

"They're not stopping for us, it's for them," Charles said, pointing at the multiple SUV's lined up on the sidewalk in front of the International Technology building. Samuel's eyes grew large as Kevin asked,

"What the hell is that?"

Charles grabbed the door handle as the team jumped out following Samuel up the stairs stopping once to flash their credentials to NYPD to get to the front entrance.

They were greeted at the security desk by a well-dressed man with a smile who pleasantly stated, "Jeffries, I thought after a lifetime of combat you would be my guy but how did you get here so fast? I sent you that email ten minutes ago." Special Agent Mallory of the SEC said, ushering the team to the back lobby. As they walked Jeffries answered, "Mallory I'll check the email but I need to get my team up to the 46th floor to talk to Audrey Burkes, one of the VP's,"-

Agent Mallory responded, "I hope that you guys at least stopped for something to eat in your haste. Miss Burkes won't be talking to anyone ever again. That's why I emailed you, she was the center of one of our largest whistleblower investigations and was found dead in her office this morning."

Samuel and the entire team responded with a collective "What?"

Mallory continued, "Look guys I gotta figure out whether or not I have to keep pursuing this whistleblower case as a retaliation homicide or will the SEC be kissing the asses of the entire board of directors of

International Technology. Take a look at your phone Samuel, I've never seen such a unique chess table."

Samuel opened his email as Mallory continued,

"Full disclosure guys, her body is halfway to the Medical Examiner's by now. She was found skewered to her chair with a Katana from her own bookshelf; whomever did this was a professional. He obviously kept her attention with a gun but the placement of the blade was precise. He went in between her third and fourth rib straight through the heart, she probably went from crying to dead in seconds. Jeffries we have no suspects, this assailant is like smoke- there are no camera angles that pick up anyone out of place and it's overcoat and hat season in NYC so there are no faces on any elevator recordings. You're looking at the only clue we have for Ms. Burkes demise."

Samuel looked at the photo in Mallory's email then handed his phone back to Sarah and the team huddled around it, Samuel put his hand on Mallory's shoulder,

"Old friend you'll be needing to work on that pucker, that chess piece is definitive evidence that Miss Burkes was on the wrong side of the law and it also answers our questions. How long until you have everything?"

"I can have everything downloaded before you guys get back to Washington."

"Tell you what, can you send it to Cynthia's laptop? We're headed over to 57th to try to talk to her stockbroker boyfriend Joey Malcolm."

"Jeffries we've got units at his penthouse right now and whatever information he had, I assure you he gave up. He took two 10mm rounds to the mouth after what appears to be a micro explosion that ripped into his hands, I assume he's collateral damage in the killer's hunt for Audrey." Mallory said

A defeated Samuel shook his hand, "Thanks, Mallory."

Sarah sent pictures of the chess table to her phone and handed Samuel's phone back to him. She walked directly to the SUV that was now causing a small grid lock and climbed into the 3rd row focused on the pictures. Samuel and team said their goodbyes to Mallory and loaded into the Chevy. Cynthia opened her laptop, set it on the dash and begin to type but it was Sarah that broke the silence,

"Who the hell is this guy? I just found her yesterday!"

Kevin in total agreement with Sarah, "Brussia let loose a psychopath and now he's off the leash."

Samuel thought about the details and started, "No, we want him to be a psychopath because there's a strategic plan in our textbooks to catch one. Snitch was smart enough to pick up the pawn and replace it with his sniper round and never leave a print. Tie that with the skilled utilization of Audrey's own authentic silent weapon on display and Snitch becomes a complex subject that we know nothing about. That's beyond smart."

Sarah blurted, "Somebody's helping him. No matter how smart he is, somebody's got to be helping him. He put the sniper round directly in front of the king on the chest table as if he were telling us checkmate."

Samuel, pulling into the hanger responded, "He put that round on the chess table intentionally and the precision in which he used that Katana shows us that he is skilled in weapons. It says he can kill silently with or without a rifle but he takes full credit. He is showing his versatility. Snitch is telling us that if we are looking for just a sniper shot we are severely mistaken."

"Wait a minute, Brussia just cut off the money supply to Mickell, who does that? That's a horrible move." Charles stopped as he turned to the G6. "It was a smart thing to do because she showed up on the radar." Sarah said. "The SEC obviously had frozen her international accounts during the final phase of the investigation. Brussia would know once Burk's was under the microscope of SEC they were going to find everything. It makes sense to get rid of the risk and with Eugene gone you have no reason to stay in hiding. Why not just eliminate any paper trail that Audrey may leak during SEC questioning."

Cynthia chimed in, "Snitch left that round in replace of the E2 pawn."

"Play a lot of Chess Cynthia?" Samuel chuckled.

"Not at all but I've watched every chess game that Frank played at least a dozen times. The King's pawn to E4 was the first move Frank made every single game in retention. Snitch put his sniper round there for a reason."

That custom hand carved chess table with Jade pieces was missing the E2 pawn. A shiny, hand crafted AX-50 sniper round in its place. Since it was first fired 2 1/2 years ago into the chest of Frank Fregoso, it's maintained its velocity in front of the team as they found themselves perplexed in the chase of an assailant only known as Snitch.

Cynthia's headphones filled the jet cabin repeating the only two words recorded from Frank Fregoso's detainment. Cynthia removed one of her earbuds, "Frank only said 2 words the entire time he was locked away but it only took the Portugal embassy an hour to have his private attorney at the door of the facility in Colorado. That is planning all the events of your death. Frank was the head of the organization because he never failed to see every possibility for his organization. The mistake Brussia has made is he's not Frank. He can't run the organization as well as Frank did."

Sarah smiled, "Cindy's right. Fregoso was a genius, let's face it, fifty years of perfection. His first Interpol picture we took less than 3 years back. That's King! It's time to get intimate with this organization and I mean it, it's time to relook at Frank. There's no criminal organization in the world that we track and monitor that has remained this stealth for decades, the Fregoso organization maybe better than we are and I'm not fucking okay with that. We need to get caught up on their playbook."

"We've got about 20 minutes before we touchdown, where do we start," Samuel asked?

Charles interjected, "We start with what happened to the boyfriend Joey Malcolm. This poor bastard doesn't live with Audrey or work with her but they're in on the same case. He's whistleblowing garbage and he gets his hands damn near blown off and two 10mm rounds into his mouth. Hell, Eugene got less of a punishment and he had keys to the front door of the organization. Plus, if you can dispatch and steal federally a protected witness why would you need to kill a boyfriend for information?"

Charles was right and the team hit the FBI headquarters in Washington eager to find out why, only to see Director Murphy in their huddle room fully engaged in the SEC findings sent a head of them by Special Agent Mallory.

The team entered the huddle room to see Director Murphy picking up a red marker and move beside the whiteboard with the Fregoso organization outlined.

"Team please take a seat, I took the Liberty of making copies of everything sent from New York. We're still waiting on the autopsy report from the high rise but with that exception everything is here. I know that you've had a long hour to think about what transpired this morning and I promise we will get there. First, I would like for you to allow me to give you some good news."

Director Murphy crossed out Frank Fregoso's face followed by Eli Eugene.

"Ladies and gentlemen congratulations! The Fregoso organization has taken a solid hit and two of FBI's top 10 have been eliminated. Your pressure saved the SEC what might have been one of the costliest whistleblower mistakes in history against International Technology. Justice will be served properly but let's not overlook the justice in these animals dispatching each other."

The team understood Murphy's point of view and focused attentively on the Director.

"Audrey Burks was one hell of a find Sarah. Your due diligence in sticking with the financial avenues established after Frank was assassinated allowed you to navigate through a very well-hidden financial maze. The return on the payment in Russia was under so many layers that alerts would have never sounded. Burkes and her boyfriend confirms that Snitch is a very skilled and highly intelligent human being. We know this because he put a bullet in Frank Fregoso's heart behind two layers of glass in a place no one on earth was supposed to know existed. That's a contract that comes with a death sentence unless you have planned every second of your life and carry an advantage through your skill level. An advantage that ensures no one would come after you. He's expensive and a man that expensive knows no loyalties to his employers. This makes Snitch dangerous in their world but gives us a chance in ours. His sniper round on Audrey's chess table let us know his price. Audrey and her boyfriend were worth $125- billion dollars to Brussia. The SEC was simply investigating, they did not freeze her offshore accounts. It was closed in person by Martin Groshki at a branch in Panama 2-days ago."

Samuel looked at the table to see the teams faces as Director Murphy dropped yet another bomb of bad news. There was anguish, concern, and anger in everyone, along with a small bit of hope coming from Cynthia. Samuel put his hand up in a motion that told the team to hold their emotions in with their opinions and allow the director to proceed.

"Team criminal organizations don't fall, they evolve. We all know that it would have taken all the Fregoso organization's power to accomplish something like Florida after assassinating Frank. Aiden Gina has been quiet and Martin has been on the move bouncing between London and Brazil. Samuel you and your team have brought down a nice slice of the upper echelon of the Fregoso organization.

All of Martin's activity tells me there's turmoil at the top and we just need to make sure that we're prepared with a full fledge assault for the winner of this power struggle. It's going to be bloody because there are a lot of politicians that are finding themselves worried. Worried that their secret alliances that were guarded by Frank won't be honored by the new leader and that opens up lots of doors for men like Gina and Brussia."

He looked around at the agents in the room before he began again.

"Now entertain me for a moment as we work together to expose another twist, I would like to add as we digest what happened in New York. Aiden Gina is the closest thing to Frank's predecessor that we, and the Central Intelligence Agency can come up with period. Vero Brussia doesn't make the top five. New York was definitely a statement but the question is, who's statement? Snitch is a hired assassin and neither one of his employers understand loyalty. They'll give him up if we squeeze them hard enough and the reconstruction of the Fregoso organization will give us the opportunity to catch them making mistakes and bring them to justice. Remember in doing so, we will provide an old man that found his end in our care a little respect and still cripple the empire that he built."

Just then something came through on Charles' laptop.

"Yes Charles. Why are you raising your hand?" Director Murphy chuckled as he rubbed his eyes, "We just got the corner's report for Joey Malcolm and confirmation on the new king."

The entire team looked at Charles as he read the words from his laptop. The 10mm rounds that killed Eli Eugene in Florida were fired from the same gun that ended Malcolm, solidifying Snitch as our only assailant. The almost impressive thing is that Joey Malcolm is not a match for the DNA of the man found in the high rise even though the door man, two neighbors and SEC agents positively identified the remains."

"Who the hell was he?" Director Murphy asked.

Charles responded, "We knew him as the name we assigned, Carl Stephanie but the Autopsy report identified him as Lorenzo Aldredge."

"Christ!" Director Murphy turned to the board crossed out Lorenzo Aldredge and sat down shocked with the rest of the team.

Cynthia stood up looking at the board and placed the picture of Audrey's Chess table down, you're right, Sir."

Director Murphy looked up as she continued.

"Snitch is brilliant. He shot Lorenzo twice in the mouth and shredded his hands so that we would know. Just like that damn chest table, he wanted the FBI to know it was him. These are contract kills- there's no reason to sign every death, plus these crumbs are only messages for the FBI. No one else would have a clue about it. Snitch wanted us to know that Lorenzo Aldredge was 100% accounted for."

"If Gina has the leash to Snitch how the hell do we stop him? Samuel asked. Director Murphy turned to Samuel.

"Stop him? We can't stop Snitch! Not directly. We have to follow the leash to the hand that's holding it. Martin was in Panama and given our current status with that country, there's a good chance Gina was there too. Martin is the one that is arrogantly public so when he gets into a country where we have friends, we take him down."

Chapter 10

Looking up at the apple securely clenched in the jaws of the concrete lion protecting all words spoken in the Capitol at the Chamber Palace of Nicholas the 1st, an older man smiled as Snitch greeted him. They embraced and sat quietly as their coffee was served. The older gentleman thanked the attendant and began to speak to Snitch as the door closed.

"My young friend I remember your father and I sitting here the year you were placed into the Academy. He said he would change the way this country thought about its disregarded youth, and to my astonishment you did not just graduate-you built Vloggish from the cold black stones of the Siberian winter. Your 'Babulya' once spoke to the ancestors of the Lion, Nicholas the 1st and advised that not all our country's history would be easy to endure. This country's loyalty was forged through perseverance and determination and like Nicholas the 1st, I honor your family's commitment to the alliances that maintain the world's order. What may we do to assist you and your family during the transition?" He paused allowing them both to enjoy their first sip of Moscow's perfectly blended coffee.

Snitch placed the cup gently back onto the saucer. "You and this beautiful country have endured long enough. My father would be proud to call you friend and comrade and I will not ask the people of Russia to suffer one more night under the fist of tyranny. Today before the 21st changing of the guard on the Sacred Stones of the Kremlin, your citizens will once again be free to be Russian. I know the things asked of you these past 2 years put your ego into a compromising position, but it's only when our egos are humbled that we can truly focus on the absolute victory that is promised to the loyal. I raise my glass to the souls of the truly loyal, that they always be honored and that their sacrifices be made-not in vain, but martyrized in our strength and friendship."

The two men stood and embraced as they exited the capitol room down the stairs to the Chamber Palace Fourier where 33 alpha FSB elite stood with the Presidential guard. Looking down from the lion statues at the platform of the staircase the older gentleman asked Snitch, "Are you sure there is nothing I can provide you in your journey young friend?"

Snitch reached out his hand and all in attendance saluted the gentleman. He honored him with a salute and shouted in Russian, "Here's to the return of the lion and another 20 years of prosperity!" Snitch embraced the man one last time and exited the Kremlin with FSB in a convoy of KGB security vehicles blaring blue lights headed to the Moscow Novoslobodskaya station.

The metro crowd stood in a silent fear as Snitch and the soldiers made their way onto the platform, a private subway car arrived and all 34 men stepped inside. When they arrived at Dostoyevskaya station Snitch dialed into the PA system and announced in Russian "Ladies and gentlemen the station is hereby closed until tomorrow morning, please take your КРОНКА card up to the exit stall for a five thousand ruble load for your inconvenience. Thank you."

One single door opened and a fully armed soldier stepped out as the door closed behind him. The confused crowd looked at him as he exclaimed, "I will not repeat the message! Exit now."

He escorted every passenger up and out of the Metro Stop and stood post at the door.

Mickell Vosh left the foreign exchange bank with his private security at his side. The four men crossed the street walking directly to the waiting soldier at the doors of the Dostoyevskaya station. Mickell laughed to his guard, "Was I so long with that greedy manager that you called ahead?"

His head of security explained, "Sir the clearing of the station at this time of day takes time. I took the opportunity while waiting to ensure your car would not be delayed."

Mickell greeted the waiting soldier with a firm pat on the back as he and his guards walk down into the station. The doors of the private car opened as the four made their way onto the beautifully marbled floor and the remaining thirty-two Alpha FSB elite stepped out of the subway car, making a circle around Mickell Vosh as his three men joined the formation. Mickell looked around and shouted, "This is betrayal and all of you pigs will die screaming after I take care of the shadow hiding inside of my private car! I am going to take pleasure watching your families die excruciating deaths for your betrayal. You have no idea the hell from which I have risen but today you will learn my true viciousness. Now, you in my subway car too cowardly to show your face, the mind trick that you have accomplished on these men won't last long as you cower in the dark."

Snitch walked out of the private car into the circle of men to join Mickell and stated with confidence, "Your threats are warranted Mickell, but allow me to provide you the reason why these men stand loyal".

Mickell smiled, "Entertain me before your death, if you must."

Snitch pointed over Mickell's left shoulder, "Just outside of this beautiful city there set a small school carved into the countryside. The cold black stones that made the walls just as hard and cold as this beautiful marble station but dripping the stench of death and torture."

Mickell straighten his shoulders and squinted hard focused on every word as Snitch continued.

"You and Vero both knew this academy of hell well. Of course, now it sits on fertile land and its inhabitants are a gift to this beloved country. The once dark academy is now the source of strength for all Russian military. For those of us comrade who crawled out as warriors, when its name alone injected trembling through all Russian boys, we learned through pain and torment what these men around you have been bred to honor through loyalty. You plotted to kill Frank Fregoso and have put your own kinsmen in peril."

For the first time in their conversation Mickell broke eye contact and began looking down at his feet. He rose his head and began to speak, "Vero when he's angry, is beyond the devil. He is all that is evil in both of us but he is still my brother and for that-"

Snitch interrupted Mickell, "For that you chose to die for your disloyalty."

"No, Wait!" Mickell placed his hand up with palms open, "Vero's anger is not to be taken lightly my life would have been eliminated if I did not do my part."

Snitch walked closer to Mickell, "Show me that you can die with the strength that you once lived with to become a warrior of the academy, or I will have these men gut you like a fucking pig."

Mickell squeezed his fist tight as the entire group of men around him clinched theirs. Snitched turned his back and walked towards the subway car pulling out a lone sniper round, handing it to the FSB captain he whispered, "There is no need for this country to suffer anymore, his financial arrangement will shed light on his fate upon eviction."

Snitch shook the captain's hand giving him the round, "Ensure he clinches this in his left hand when he is discovered, you and your men have honored the walls of Vloggish with your loyalty today my friend."

Snitch walked onto the subway car and as it drove away the men tightened the circle around Mickell. The percussion of the strikes to his body echoed in the empty walls of the metro station as his bones begin to break from the abuse that had become the punishment for his disloyalty.

Chapter 11

Senior agent Kevin Goodson had exhausted every foreign resource across Russia he had worked so carefully over the years to build, and was still sitting empty-handed. The phone rang, an old friend a Russian intelligence was on the other line. He had been recently stonewalled by his own military and reached out to Kevin because he needed help on a local police case that discovered Mickell Vosh's body. Kevin quickly gathered everything his source could provide and called the team to the huddle room.

Charles led the team in to see Kevin put a red "X" across the face of Mickell Vosh on the seven man pyramid that was once the engine of the Fregoso organization. Charles blurted, "What's good Goodson?"

"Russian police found Vosh's body."

The team sat down as Kevin loaded one of the only two pictures his source was able to send to him. They looked at the body of Mickell Vosh lying naked in the middle of a king size hand-carved mahogany bed. His body was riddled with deep purple bruises and his legs and torso showed clear signs of broken bones trying to protrude through the dead man's flesh.

Kevin continued, "The official report from the Russian government is that Vosh was secretly hiding in Moscow with the assistance of an American - Audrey K Burks, and when Miss Burks stop paying for the Moscow Villa, the body of Mickell Vosh was discovered when a legal eviction was executed. It was determined that Mickell's official time of death was mid-afternoon four days ago- just two days before the eviction was signed. His official cause of death is said to be natural causes."

When Kevin paused, it was a race to outburst first, that Sarah won by milliseconds as she raised her voice slightly to make sure everyone heard her over the rest, "The only way that poor bastard died from natural causes is if Russia considers being hit by a damn 18- wheeler head on to be natural. What the hell?"

Cynthia and Charles laughed.

Kevin what is he gripping in his hand?" Cynthia asked.

Senior agent Goodson took a deep breath causing an uncomfortable silence in the room, "That's the only reason I got the intel. My guy called and said Mickell was found dead, and the military had confiscated all evidence from the eviction, and they were closing the case. He said he was sending me this photo of Vosh in exchange for help identifying the round found in his hand."

Kevin changed the picture to show evidence from the Russian intelligence of one of Snitch's A X 50 sniper rounds.

Samuel sat back in his chair and whispered silently to himself, "Gina's holding the leash."

Charles got everyone's attention, "Snitch had this done and it wasn't just because Aiden Gina and Martin Groshki paid him-this was sanctioned by officials high up. You guys remember how much damn red tape we had to go through with Lorenzo's testimony and the Russian military to get the green light on an aging mafia. There's no way he died in that room- it's too catastrophic. That means he was killed and transported across Moscow. No way that happens without his own men catching you unless you've got the military assistance."

Kevin answered his speculation, "Charles I'd love to be able to confirm or even deny that, but the entire European continent seems to be, almost suspiciously, minding their own damn business right now."

"He wanted us to know it was him. He is making sure that we understand there's a clear and very pronounced path that he is following. It leads straight to him but right now I don't think any of us speak the language. That leaves us with a room of facts and misunderstandings," Samuel said, standing as he remembered what Murphy said about there being justice in allowing the rats to exterminate one another.

"None of us need to speak the language, we need to understand what's going on with the Fregoso organization and the rules they play by. Focusing on Snitch and that damn sniper round has clearly led us nowhere for the better part of 3 years. Instead, we are going to focus all of our energy on the people who paid to awaken Snitch's violet talents. That's Vero Brussia and Aiden Gina. Since we know Mickell Vosh found out that his side lost in Moscow, we need to assume somewhere here state side the next on the org chart to die is walking around oblivious. If we find Brussia, we find our shooter because Gina is going to kill him. We got to figure out where Brussia is and perhaps we save his ass from being assassinated and lock them both up for the rest of their lives."

Chapter 12

Vero Brussia sat at the bar of a breathtaking luxury golf resort in New Jersey. The location had over one-thousand suites that included first class amenities and fifty private waterfront cottages- everything the future bride and groom would want or desire. He started to address a battle proven, eager young man- the only other person at the bar besides the bartender.

"My friend, tonight I wish you and your bride-to-be one-thousand years of happiness through your children and theirs. I want you to enjoy your honeymoon but know this, once you return she will need to understand that she is married to the new right hand of the Fregoso organization. There will be lonely months as you rebuild and realign everything that Eli destroyed with his bastardize betrayal and once that's accomplished, you and your beautiful bride will live better in this country than that coward of a president these greedy fucking people follow a-"

He paused, smiling at the incoming text that satiated his rage and chuckled. "But today," He started again as he rose his glass to his new Lieutenant and motioned for the bartender to bring another round.

"Mickell and the organization celebrate with you. They sent your wedding gift early by paying for all of the accommodations and ensuring that this weekend we will be surrounded by only family."

The young man smiled and finished his drink after toasting, "Vero, I won't let you down, and when I return, I plan on reestablishing stronger ties with North and South America. I consider it an honor to be here today having learned from the examples you and Mickell provide and knowing all the lessons the two of you have taught me will pave the way for a new organization and it drives me to prove and demonstrate my loyalty in all my actions."

Brussia laughed looking down at the text message, "Save that energy for your young bride, tonight is a true celebration! I must take this, I will see you tonight to toast to our new family."

Brussia left his new Lieutenant incredibly pleased. He climbed into the rented Hummer and drove up the private road to his waterfront cottage, smiling, looking down at the message on his phone again. It read 'I have arrived with a gift', it was more enjoyment than he could take. Brussia left the room key in the slot as his excitement bubbled to the surface when he opened the door. He could see the light on in the grand dining room and hurried his pace inside. In the center of the dining room stood a huge hand carved mahogany table with seating for ten, and at the end seat, sat Snitch with his jacket folded neatly across the arm of the massive chair. Vero, seeing Snitch sitting calmly, smiled as his eyes quickly found their target. A cold bottle of clear liquid sealed with two crystal glasses, a manila folder and a blue gift box all staged beautifully at the head of the table for Vero.

Sitting with a smile Vero said, "My friend, you really are worth your weight in gold. This bottle of vodka is from an independent family outside of Moscow. I always pick one up when I make it home. Where did you find this?"

"Outside of Moscow, my friend." Snitch replied.

You brought this for me? Thank you, I am assuming with your abundance of gifts there was no problem with the transfers."

"No Mr. Brussia, perhaps a toast." Snitch quickly suggested.

Vero laughed, "First we confirm all rumors my friend." He tapped the bottle and then picked up the manilla folder. "I knew when you took care of Frank you were worth every penny you asked for."

Brussia opened the folder. There were three color photos: the first, Pauline Lucy, dead in the sand. He chuckled. "She didn't deserve to wear white, lying whore."

He flipped to the next picture and his dark eyes brightened. "Eli, I trusted you, but you sir," He smiled looking up at Snitch, "you have done the unthinkable. You have freed me, allowing me to fulfill my destiny. I would have preferred his heart in that box, but his throat will do."

He opened the box to see Eli Eugene's perfectly preserved esophagus then put the top back on. Snitch smiled, "Sir I believe the message that was sent in Orlando carried more meaning to everyone in the Fregoso organization than having his heart in that box."

Brussia smiled again, "You are right but still, his heart would have been pleasing."

Then he whispered in Russian, "Treachery should be punished more brutally in public so that all can learn."

Snitch quickly replied in Russian as well, startling Brussia, "For we all must remain loyal until the end."

The two men continued their conversation speaking in Russian.

"Your Russian is better than mine, my friend."

"Thank you Comrade. When was the last time you were home?"

Vero aggressively snapped, "It's been many years, and you? When was the last you visited my home young man?"

Breaking their eye contact for the first time Snitch looked down at the manila folder in Vero's hand, "Just yesterday Mr. Brussia."

Vero hesitatingly looked down to the picture of Eli's body and flipped it slowly to see Mickell's devastatingly brutalized body lying on the brilliant black and stone marbled floor in the middle of Dostoyevskaya metro station. Brussia's rage rose his head and filled his body, his skin turned a dark red as he began to tunnel his anger and seethe. Snitch rose the 10mm 1911 and fired two rounds into his chest, the tranquilizers ravaged his bloodstream never allowing Brussia's words to be released as his head landed soundly on the wooden table.

Snitch rubbed his face with his free hand and took a deep breath before placing the gun gently on the table. He sat back in the chair and said softly to Brussia, "My brother, you have allowed the darkness to rule your soul.

Four hours later Vero Brussia blinked his eyes as he started to gain consciousness, he was still at the head of the table, the chair pushed in snugly with the table against his abdomen. His eyes began to focus between his hands as he saw the charred, black, hand polished handle of a beautiful hatchet. Just under the bulky hammer head of the weapon sat a new railroad spike. Brussia's instinct was to jump to his feet and a small panic coursed through his veins when his attempts to move where denied. He was fastened to the table with slotted metal ribbon screwed directly into the tabletop across his wrist and elbows with his hands facing down. Unable to move anything but his shoulders Vero made the shocking discovery that his feet were not on the ground, but the table was holding him in that position. His legs were secured to the base of the large hand carved table with the same metal ribbon, secured above and below his knees and at his ankles. Small chills ran across Brussia's back when his chin bumped the ball gag loosely sitting around his neck and he quickly rose his head to see the display at the opposite end of the table. His eyes widened as he looked down the beautiful mahogany grains leading to the end seat where the opened bottle of vodka and one crystal glass set. A thumb of the clear liquid with a sniper round sitting straight up inside. Vero knew the deadly pour as the sign that his death had been sanctioned by all of Russia. The color left his face and for the first time in ages Vero Brussia feared for his future as Snitch entered the dining room.

(Both men speaking in Russian)

"You cowardice lying son of bitch! You will bleed for this! Your skull will be crushed under the boot heels of vengeance." Brussia yelled.

Snitch walked directly to Vero placing both of his hands on his right forearm, "The adrenaline spike that occurs when the sedative wears off is what's causing you not to evaluate your current circumstance logically. The belief that your threats mean anything at this moment will soon give way to the reality of your determination. I assure you brother, all of Russia sleeps well knowing tomorrow you will be no more. You climbed out of a hell that was designed to torment and break you and you became a true power under the tutelage of Frank Fregoso but you returned with all your power and all your influence and did nothing! The administrator you left behind learned a lesson from you Vero, never remove the handle from the hatchet. It is dangerous, it allows the child to believe he can find victory in his strength and anger."

Brussia looked down at the hatchet calmly, "Something tells me you are not worthy of these tools. You are simply a paid assassin but there's no sniper rifle at this table. I found my life in that death camp and you are not even worth the rusty barbed wire that riddles the land! You're going to have to look me in my eyes and determine if your soul will allow you to risk what will happen to you when that hatchet falls. In the end, will you be able to complete what you have been paid to do young man?"

Snitch took his hands off the man's arm and turned around walking to the end of the table unbuttoning his shirt. A strong chiseled body covered in deep scars stood at the end chair as he placed his shirt across the hand carved arm. One injury in particular made Vero's attitude and complexion vanish simultaneously. It was seven inches long lining

Snitch's shoulder blade and creating a rugged straight line that churned the brutal gangster's stomach. A fear and finality that Vero Brussia could only remember feeling one other time in his life.

"The gag was never to stop your mouth Vero." Snitch stared. "It's only now that you realize there is a beautiful darkness that will be satiated by taking your life for all that have suffered. There's a hunger for loyalty that you don't possess and you fail to understand that those who serve must serve loyally. Frank Fregoso was loyal to you through his last breath, and you repaid him with betrayal and today you will die because of that betrayal."

Snitch turned and walked back to Vero, grabbing the ball gag in his fist. He looked into the once boastful eyes of Vero Brussia asking, "Is there anything you have left inside brother?"

Vero lowered his eyes giving no fight as Snitch locked the gag in his mouth.

"You will be a message to all that disloyalty has severe consequences."

He grabbed the railroad spike, placed it on top of Brussia's right hand and clinched the hatchet tight. "You were Frank Fregoso's violent angel and you betrayed him."

Brussia began to bite into the ball gag screaming. Snitch rose the hammer side of the hatchet high into the air as Vero's hand could only claw at the mahogany frantically, it landed solid onto the head of the railroad spike. The blow pierced Brussia's hand crushing bones, bursting blood vessels and tapping into the hardwood. Snitch released the spike looking into Brussia's eyes as his cries of anguish reverberated through out the premises. The piercing distinct sound of teeth cracking into the ball gag was drowned out by nails scraping slivers of mahogany deep inside his nail bed as he saw Snitch raise his hand again. Vero cried out "No!" through the gag but Snitch answered his plea by lowering his hand, with all his might, slamming the hammer head of the hatchet directly onto the railroad spike again. The wood splintered as the railroad spike seeded itself into the table, dragging bits of Vero's tendons with it. Brussia's teeth lay buried deep inside of the ball gag as he screamed in pain and agony to no avail. Snitch placed the hatchet onto the table and walked behind Vero. Panicking, Vero swung his head as far as possible to see Snitch pick up a one foot long by one-inch thick industrial zip tie. He walked around to Vero's arm and slid the zip tie under his Armani suit and fastened it securely around Vero's forearm.

"The tourniquet will allow you to reflect on your disloyalty and the anguish that your selfish anger brought to thousands."

On the verge of unconsciousness, the hardened killer found himself disgusted with the rejuvenation that the sudden halt to his bleeding provided. Snitch waited patiently for his screams to subside as the pain continued to course through Vero's body, then he picked up the hatchet and climbed onto the table and took a knee in front of Vero.

"My friend, it's not punishment if you have not given the forsaken time to reflect on the disloyalty they have committed allowing them to see the treachery in their ways."

Vero Brussia rose his eyes as Snitch rose the hatchet high above his head. The words ripped through Brussia's memories, landing decades ago the first time he heard Frank say it to a man that like him now deserved Frank's reckoning. Tears fell freely from his eyes as he embraced the punishment his disloyalty demanded. The hatchet slammed into his shoulder severing Vero's collarbone and driving deep into his sternum, coming to a grinding stop as the blade and the back of Brussia's wooden chair met with a thump. Vero Brussia's fight diminished as his body embraced the pain and death began to tighten its clutch as his blood flowed. Snitch stood and stepped down from the table watching the dying man.

"Vloggish will never speak of you nor Mickell in the light of loyalty ever again. From now through eternity you will be the final headmaster and here, you will die for your disloyalty to the Fregoso Family."

***

The entire resort was sparkling with excitement as the Groom addressed his bride and all in attendance.

"My uncle Frank was the 26th generation of Francisco Fregoso. He gave a toast at a family gathering once and I would like to honor him, and my lovely bride by carrying on Uncle Frank's toast."

It was quite simple.

"To love from one's soul is to be loyal to that love through eternity. Today I make that promise of love to you."

He looked at his bride then to the crowd with glasses high, he said. "Obrigado."

Chapter 13

The team sat in the VIP conference room on the main premises of the resort. Four of the conference rooms and the entire Brussia cottage had been completely converted into makeshift huddle rooms and evidence processing centers. The team tried to focus on where to start.

"Charles," What's Kevin's ETA?"

"Goodson was in New York only 40 minutes out- that was 25 minutes ago so he's either here and making his way to us or pretty damn close."

Samuel accepted the response and questioned, "What do we know so far?"

Sarah chimed, "This entire resort was bought and paid for by Audrey Burkes six months ago. She paid for the resort's all inclusive, exclusive weekend that comes with a million-dollar damage waiver and 80% occupancy charge. The wedding party and all staff was meant to be completely private. The only person we have on camera is Brussia when he pulls up Friday morning and then all the cameras go off. The crime scene was cleaned and there's a chance he was dead before the wedding but there's not much to work with. Nothing has yielded prints of any kind, but this place was booked for a wedding and we have no idea whose. It takes a lot of money to pull this off."

"Power!" Sr. Agent Goodson walked into the conference room breathing as if he ran the entire way. "The drink was the final determination, it's an agreed upon sentencing and that pour with Snitch's round says Russia wanted this to happen and I missed it-I completely missed it"

"Goodson slow down, what the hell did you miss?" Charles asked.

"I couldn't see it with Mickell. I didn't see it clearly-it didn't make sense until today. Brussia's death strike was exactly like the headmaster from the academy's last graduating class. The one that gave birth to what we know as the Alpha-Elite training ground for Russia's top military, Vloggish."

Kevin paused as Sarah's face announced her outburst.

"You mean that shit was true? Those poor fucking tortured children."

"One of those poor tortured children grew up to be Vero Brussia." Samuel replied.

Kevin grabbed the team's attention again, "I didn't see why everyone was so silent but now I see that Brussia and Mickell have no political connections outside of Russia. All the information they had came from their connections through their power inside of Russia. Vero had no idea this was coming. They kept Burkes and Lorenzo a secret from him, just like Mickell's demise, this thing was orchestrated beautifully. Money trails off with Audrey and no witnesses that were not loyal to Frank Fregoso. Brussia was blindsided because it was sanctioned by Vloggish, and that old bottle of vodka with a single poor with a round in it, is the sign. It's called "The Final Determination".

In the time of Nicholas the 1st, it was customary for high-ranking members of the military to be brought to trial for their miss doings. There would be no court just a firing squad. At the wall would stand a glass of vodka, if you were found guilty it would be your last pour because a round would be in the glass. If you were found not guilty it became the best drink of your life and your loyalty would be solidified."

Kevin took a seat giving his attention to Cynthia, "For the non-Russian folklore agent, Vloggish is?"

"Vloggish is an abandoned Cold War project turned state-of-the-art military training ground. K2, the Kremlin's secondary fallout, in case of a World War-it's an exact replica of the Kremlin in the middle of nowhere. It has running water, electricity and gas lines and there's also a huge abandoned rock query said to be a fully functional missile base only 30 miles south." Kevin answered.

"We know the facility well Goodson. Sarah and I both trained there with the Alphas for grid search tactical, as far as training facilities go it's amazing." Charles replied.

"I understand that guys and I've trained there too. Did you notice that every time you've ever gone to train there, the exact same buildings are set for demolish but they look damn near perfect?"

Charles and Sarah looked at each other as the same light bulb went off in their heads as Kevin continued.

"The place has a building that is flooded on the inside for deep water rescues that doesn't leak on the outside. Those buildings set to be demolished are all the living quarters and they have been blocked off for years. Every situation that they put together in that place is picture perfect. Hell, even the children in the urban scenarios are rock solid and they create better than some of our own soldiers."

"Those kids that were running the drills for us as teen shooters didn't flinch-they knew that place like the back of their damn hands," Sarah sparked. "Holy hell, Charles! That's why we died every damn time we tried to wait out for rescue, we were playing at their house. I guarantee you there's a direct route to that damn rock query under the snow."

Cynthia only took a moment to get inoculated in Vloggish history before drawing the full picture and she stood up,

"Which is why there's no Intel coming in- Gina had full military and political approval, but it doesn't explain why Snitch needed to turn Brussia into the proof that the boogie man exists."

"Unless Snitch is the Dark Czar and wanted to prove it. Vloggish wasn't first, the academy was a place for wayward boys originally; said to be just on the outskirts of K2 and to our knowledge that puts its original location in that rock query. Any orphaned child or criminal minor would be sent there and the headmaster of this academy was treacherous. They only employed two men at a time to turn thousands of young boys into rugged, mindless soldiers. The headmaster and administrator were horrible and the level of abuse they inflicted on these kids was said to be beyond cruelty. They were getting rich making mercenaries against their will and this shit went on for decades. Somewhere around a decade or so ago, one of the boys killed the headmaster so violently the administrator bowed down. From that violence, it's said that Vloggish was born, the academy was turned into a school of love and nurturing for these men and they grew to be warriors. Vloggish produces some of the best soldiers in the world and the young man that took down the headmaster was given the name Dark Czar. He repeated converting places like this across different continents building his army, but this is where it started." Kevin explained. "The legend says that It was a hatchet into his clavicle through his shoulder and chest that brought the headmaster to his knees. A hatchet hand forged and made at the school, but unfortunately it didn't kill the headmaster. This Dark Czar turned to all the boys in the assembly and promised if they were loyal, they would always be considered the best of Mother Russia and the true reward of being warriors would be theirs. That was enough to ignite the years of mistreatment and all of the young men in the hall beat the man to death as he bled out."

Cynthia leaned back in her chair. "Mickell's body was beat to death."

"That would explain why everything is so business as usual since Frank." Kevin replied.

Samuel walked silently to the Fregoso organization's chart and put an "X" across Vero Brussia's face, "Team, I don't care what the hell his name is- Snitch, The Dark Lord, or The Last Kaiser, right now it's time to stop chasing rumors! We've got nothing on him after three years and no one's going to give us anything. The damn underworld has been running like a well-oiled machine for three years and Jesus, it's like Frank is still running this damn thing!"

Samuel's frustration stopped with childlike enthusiasm. "Technically Frank is still running the organization-anybody can be violent, right? You must be a political genius and have all the right ties to pull this off. Let's state the obvious ladies and gentlemen, Aiden Gina just dispatched two of the most powerful men in Russian history with permission from the Kremlin, he's taken full control of the Fregoso organization."

Charles turned towards Samuel, "Snitch was always working for him, brains and muscle on the same accord. Martin has insured none of his political power has faltered and Gina has decisively won the war. He has enough power to come out of hiding regardless of allegations. Seriously, who in their right mind would testify against that guy with an avenger like Snitch?"

Chapter 14

Samuel walked into the office to see a smiling, energetic Jason Murphy.

"Have a seat, Samuel."

Samuel sat and forced a smile, "I'm glad you're having a good day Jason."

"You need to be having a good day too, Samuel. It's time to reflect on the accomplishments our organization has made because of you and your team."

"Why is that Jason? Because I don't feel like we've accomplished a damn thing. I drug my best agents to California to set up Frank and have been leading them down a road of disappointment ever since."

Director Murphy relaxed his shoulders, "Samuel your team has been working relentlessly to dismantle the Fregoso Organization. That work has netted the removal of five people from the FBI's most wanted and decimated the leadership of the stricture down to just two men.Two men to juggle the entire arms race of the world. AD Jeffries that's a major accomplishment; your team saved the SEC from a loosing battle against International Tech! The problem is no one can see it-chasing Snitch. Samuel, you have to assume that he's a very rich man with no reason to step out of the shadows. We will decide where the FBI's best will focus when you and your team return.

"Jason where are we going?"

"Vacation!"

"Vacation?" Jeffries eyes got big as his frustration rose.

"Yes vacation, your team needs to be rewarded for their accomplishments. You and your team have been given a bonus two-week vacation and considerable raises effective immediately."

"Thank you Boss." Samuel shook his head. "I guess we've been chasing this guy so long it's easy to forget that we've taken some bad people out of society but Jason, I desperately feel like I need to understand Frank a little more."

"Then tell your team it's vacation time and decide what to pack for Portugal." Murphy shot back.

Samuel reluctantly walked out of the Director's office and down the hallway. Murphy could see the team members jump up with relief from the huddle room table and clear out without hesitation as Samuel smiled and made his way back into his office.

Late that afternoon Deputy Director John Tanner closed his door and dialed in a code to his phone. An aide answered, "Please hold Mr. Tanner."

A few moments later a man's voice calmly asked, "How can I help you Deputy Director?"

"Tom what the hell are we doing? Brussia gone gives total control to Gina! The whole damn team just left the building and they are all headed to Fregoso hot spots!"

"Tanner we aren't doing anything," The voice on the other end responded. "I am aware that the Fregoso organization is now two men instead of seven. The FBI is doing a wonderful job of cleaning up the most wanted list and allowing Aiden Gina and that gorilla he calls a right hand to hold all the keys to the one game we must play. How long do you think it's going to be before he's bold enough to come back to the mainland? His power is not split seven ways anymore. I suggest you find a way to revoke some of his travel privileges; Aiden is only a threat if he's allowed to move freely and Martin is just an arrogant bull that can be put down if he refuses to play ball."

"And Snitch?" Tanner asked.

"He's a gun for hire John, when Aiden is done with him he will crawl back into the hole he came from. His fight isn't with us, worry about Aiden and make sure Goodson doesn't leave Chicago empty handed."

The phone went dead before Tanner could retort.

***

Jason Murphy looked up to see Samuel standing in his door, go-bag in hand. "That's not luggage Samuel."

"I just-"

"You just what," Director Murphy interrupted? "Thank you for asking permission Samuel, but the rest of your team left with their go bags already so while you're trying to learn who Frank was, enjoy Portugal- it's beautiful."

"I just want answers." Samuel looked defeated.

"Try to have some fun Jeffries."

"Thanks Murphy."

***

Sarah and Charles leaned against the ladder of the G6 waving at a shocked Cynthia as she pulled into the hangar.

"What took you so long rookie?" Charles smiled.

"Y'all are really doing this?" Cynthia asked, looking a little flustered.

"Only way to get ahead of this guy is to start at the beginning."

"We owe this to Frank," Sarah said with a forced smile. "if we can find something that sheds more light on catching the bastards that murdered him maybe I'll rest better. Now more than ever I feel like the only person who understood what the hell honor is was probably that man. Our brains have a lot more information loaded and you've got fresh eyes Cindy, so I'm putting my money on you lady."

Cynthia grabbed her climbing gear and suitcase as she walked past the two of them, "Then why are we sitting here on the ground?"

Charles grabbed the remaining luggage, "My thoughts exactly!"

"Let me guess, Kevin is meeting us there?" Cynthia asked.

Charles closed the door of the cabin after confirmation with the pilot, "Goodson left the parking garage grumbling something to the effect of, "*If Russia is going to give him the silent treatment, then Chicago owes him answers."* Think he's pulling his "Untouchables" routine down in Chi-Town."

"Nice!" Cynthia giggled. "Technically, we're all on vacation and this damn thing has a stocked bar we never get to use, how about we toast to Kevin's adventure and whatever boss-man does when he's off? Of course, he's been working since he hired me into the unit."

"He had his passport out and I imagine there were no Bermuda shorts in his bag." Sarah confirmed.

"I guess that makes it unanimous," Cindy said smiling at the tray of drinks Charles was working on. "here's to finding Frank some justice."

The three raised their glasses after Charles returned from the minibar and enjoyed the remainder of the trip to Colorado.

Chapter 15

The three-story office building sat naturally in the Boulder landscape, the exterior brick the same as the majority of the city- paying tribute to the University. The outside was marked like all the city buildings in Colorado with roaming guards and gates monitoring it around the clock. Although the city facility was perfectly camouflaged to look like its surrounding cityscape, it sat alone with its back to the beautiful prairie leading to the flat irons of the Rocky's. The team checked in with the agent at the front gate and entered the facility through the underground garage access. The entire building had been renovated except for three safe rooms running along the west wall of the third floor. Frank's cell sat third in line on the corner and with the investigation still open, his cell row was left as functioning interrogation suites.

The team walked into Frank's cell and Cynthia smiled. "Oh my God, what a view!" She could see acres of dense trees that painted the mountainside and in the distance, a family of hawks drifting on the up currents. "It's beautiful."

"Wow! It really is breathtaking." Sarah agreed as she admired the mountain range. "There's at least four city blocks of tree line camouflaging every damned view the cameras and guards would have had to see any of Snitch's activity."

Charles bent down to check the trajectory markings on the new cell window, "It's a good thing our guy wasn't trying to free Frank, otherwise this safe house would have fallen and all he would have needed to do is stay in his cell. It would have allowed Snitch to pick off the agents one by one as they came to retrieve him-it would have been a massacre."

Cynthia laughed, "So I guess there's no objection with me taking Frank's suite for our stay then?"

Both Sarah and Charles walked out of the cell shaking their heads and dropped their bags into the remaining two cells.

Unwilling to turn the renovated facility into a haven of take-out containers, the team jumped into the SUV to grab food and take advantage of the remaining daylight to drive and evaluate all possible routes Snitch could have chosen up to his sniper's nest. Sarah looked out the passenger window at the beautiful scattering of tall trees as they climbed elevation.

"Once we get this high there are only two roads to the trail opening that leads to the spot-it's not a very populated area, only a hand full of luxury homes. We interviewed all the homeowners and put them all under surveillance for a year and outside of the typical American family skeletons none of them had any dirt under their nails nor ties to anything Fregoso."

Sarah had spent months after Frank's assassination canvassing the city and putting together an impressive novella of a report on all of Boulder's citizens. A report Cynthia had read four times along with the cross-agency details around the Fregoso stay at the facility. She was determined to find the underlying current that Snitch was able to discover when he surfed through all the security protocols. The team made the small hike up the slightly overgrown path to the landing from which the original sniper round was released. The three sat and begin to survey the landscape with their binoculars.

Charles focused his binoculars on the facility,

"The view of the entrance to the underground parking and the southwest corner is fantastic from here- it's the perfect spot!"

"The grove blocks the other cells and according to the CIA files, at the time, the second floor was processing." Sarah added.

"The only problem is just like now and even at dusk, the building's window clarity is skewed by the sun-in the daytime, this is a very vulnerable location. We know Snitch would not have sat here in the light and it would only take a pair of enhanced night optics to bypass the one-way glass on the cells and exterior windows."

Cynthia lowered her binoculars to notice the raptors above and grabbed Charles and Sarah's attention. "Someone in this city helped him. It's been three years so they have no reason to be cautious anymore, we're going to treat this like a cold case- a holistic investigation. Allow our environment to reveal clues as to how that sniper round found its home in Frank's chest. Snitch wouldn't have stayed here to observe-it's too far away. That means he hiked to this spot nightly until he gathered enough information to optimize the time between Frank's chess games and the guard's rotations. I want to start by hiking into this spot as many ways as I can for four days and see if any of the locals notice."

Charles piped in, "I like where you're going but let's be honest, the amount of pink alone in all your gear is going to be noticed; put that with that mane of red you got and there's no way you have not been noticed Cynthia." The team laughed. "He would have to pack everything with him nightly because there's no returning for anything once that shot is fired. I'll pack my stealth strike gear and make the rotations."

"He's right," Sarah agreed. "but that may give us the control we need. Cyndi, you stand out and we need that as a control. Charles will set the pace and Cyndi you climb the route twice to his 20 and I will see what our Boulder neighbors notice."

The team made their way to the SUV and it was night before they got back into the facility.

Charles broke the silence, "Let's think about this for a second, we're standing here looking out Frank Fregoso's window and the trajectory is solid. Knowing what we know now and understanding the precision and time Snitch takes to do everything, the real question is where would he have chosen to stay? He's smart, calculated and most important, he's got no emotional connection. He's not angry and not seeking vengeance-this is just a job. A job that's going to make him one of the richest men in the world."

Cynthia sat down on the bed, "Ok, I want to be able to see every angle of this window, and from what vantage point can I avoid the sun's glare? And I use a smaller pair of enhanced optics to avoid nosey neighbors."

Charles turned off the cell light and began to study the visible residential areas through his binoculars, "The only populated area with a view sits south of the facility, from here there are only a few commercial and residential zones."

Sarah was sitting at the chess table behind Charles, she added, "If it's only 30 degrees, eliminate all industrial areas or private homes."

Charles turned the light back on, "Damn, it's that same bundle of apartments from the original investigation. We ran every leaser and interrogated every resident that lived in an apartment with any type of view of this building."

"That's okay," Cynthia said enthusiastically. "it just means we need to be focused on surveillance sweet spots that he could check remotely. Let's get some rest and get hiking at the crack of dawn, I'm anxious to see if we can be seen from the guard lookouts."

The team sat at the massive stones above the Boulder Observation Point looking down at the whole city, having lunch with the locals and tourists brave enough to hike a little. The facility sat on the horizon just south and Cynthia started walking to the edge of a large stone. She could see a substantial opening with a small natural pond with deer drinking in the trees behind the facility.

She turned to Sarah and Charles, "Snitch is not going to leave anything to chance, he would only utilize one spot-the best spot. The only angle that matches the view from his sniper's nest. He didn't move around once he found his temporary home. He stayed put once he established his base camp and didn't make trips in and out. That's why no one noticed my three trips and Charles was suspicious from day two. Let's get in the woods, we'll walk the path straight and I'm going to need you guys to humor me please."

"Cyndi, are we doing some hippie stuff?" Sarah asked smiling.

"Yes, but for good reason."

They returned to the facility and walked to the prairie behind the building.

"Okay, take your shoes off." She told them.

"You're going to explain this." Charles challenged.

"I'll explain it as we walk. The feet are working with our eyes to determine the most worn paths, these are the most comfortable to walk barefoot and by the time we get to the tree line, we will be able to instinctively find the wildlife paths through the trees in the open grove."

They moved slowly into the tree line and Sarah noticed the birds above,

"Look at that." She said pointing up. "The hawks are paying attention but they stopped calling once we got behind the tree line. No one's allowed to hike here; it's the first thing I mapped out while watching you from the guard post as you two hiked. It's very shallow and that pond ahead utilizes the sun to cast light through the trees. CIA would have caught a shadow if Snitch got too close."

They broke through to the grove to see the beautiful pond and Cynthia noted all the deer on the other side as they calmly retreated into the trees throughout one main path.

"We need to come back tonight, this is where all visibility stops and it must be the valley in the CIA report that says wildlife scattered when Apaches lit up the night sky."

The team geared up in black ops climbing gear, turned on the original lighting set up by the facility they were in three years prior, and made their way to the grove and along the pond to the other side. The team heard Sarah in their ear as she broke the silence first, once they were well into the next tree line. "The deer aren't even spooked, they're watching us like they're used to seeing the shadows moving upright."

Charles gave the signal to pause their movement, "Nothing's running away, look at that damn deer over there. Snitch used this trail a lot, he walked here."

The deer scattered from Cynthia's excitement as she yelled, "He didn't live with anyone, he lived here! He could go straight out of here, up to the sniper nest every night and never be noticed. Frank was only there for three months, which means Snitch could get a month's supply of camping rations in and only have to leave the mountain two times after that. I've lived on the side of a mountain at base camp for days- it was easy, he lived somewhere in this forest."

Sarah smiled, "Cyndi, you are one amazing hippie, I love you right now. Let's get back and hit this place hard come sunup."

The team called in every available agent in the northern Colorado area and gave instructions to sweep the grounds between the sniper location and the tree line behind the pond for any sign of human activity. They focused on the trees in the 15-degree area that follows the trajectory of Snitch's shot. Charles stopped on a worn wildlife path as he looked at a large rock sitting only two feet from a massive pine. He called out to Cynthia and Sarah, "We got to get up that tree. Snitch put that rock there, it's the only one that size this far down the mountains and here he could step off the path onto it, get up that tree and never leave a trace of human activity."

The three of them climbed up with trail magnets running on long lines (an old climber trick to find strongholds.) They climbed 175 feet- only 20 feet from the point that the pine occupied the skyline alone. There was no trace of any unnatural disturbances in the trees so the exhausted team stopped to check the status of the forest floor search. The negative response gave Sarah determination to push the last stretch.

"Guys I want to climb up to that peak, I just need to get a line up there."

"Throw my magnet line, it's on a 200-pound test." Charles informed her reeling his rope up and handing it to Sarah.

She leaned back and swung the magnet up and as it spun around the branch it stopped suddenly locking to the tree trunk, five feet below the anchoring branch Sarah picked. The loud clink gave them all the motivation to push up to the mark on the tree. Sarah was the first to lock in at the support branch and told Cynthia and Charles, "It's grown into the tree, but that is a universal stabilization lock, he could have brought anything up here."

Charles sat on the lower branch, "He slept here, it's the perfect spot and with the right camo gear all he would have to do is pull his lines up, even if you were standing on the ground looking straight up you wouldn't see his base camp. Can we get it out?"

Cynthia answered, "Not without harming the tree-it's part of it now, let's just get some pictures of it and Frank's cell from this vantage point. Jesus, what can't Snitch do?"

"He can't go into Boulder and buy a month's worth of supplies and not be on any closed-circuit camera in the city, somebody knows something." Sarah replied.

"He wouldn't have to, remember no one saw Cynthia hiking; Gina could have sent a monthly care package via backpacker and no one would've been the wiser. They wouldn't have to come all the way to the grove, they would be able to leave it somewhere up the mountain and he could go retrieve it; never making contact at all. It's fucking irritatingly perfect. Let's get out of this damn tree and see what these pictures give us." Charles said reluctantly.

Chapter 16

Cynthia walked out into the large foyer to greet the former CIA station chief that led the facility from inception to decommissioning. "Thank you for joining us Kase, Sarah and Charles are in the conference room."

They all sat and she started immediately, "Kase, why isn't there any intel from Frank Fregoso? There was no attempt at communication. No *actual* CIA work was done."

Kase took a deep breath, "At the time Mr. Fregoso was here, this facility was fully operational, that means- Ms. Prince, we never failed to get cooperation from any of our house guests." There was a tranquility in his voice.

"Then why wasn't Frank interrogated?" Charles questioned. "It was signed off by Brass."

Kase smiled as he looked out the first-floor window, "It was a 1534-H guys, in all honesty I'm not going to die in Guantánamo Bay because I interrogated a man with connections all the way up to the White House lawn."

Cynthia leaned in, "You're telling me the Secret Service considered the interrogation of Frank Fregoso a possible terroristic act? Why didn't you divulge any of this information in the files?"

Without hesitation, the veteran CIA agent quipped, "I did divulge everything in the files. Mr. Fregoso said no more then two words after asking for a cell that provided moonlight to play chess for his entire stay. The only communication he had was a daily call made to the embassy in which he did nothing but breathe. Guys, we were served notice by his embassy lawyers half an hour after he was dropped off by your team. They advised that no attempts to challenge our charges pending Pauline Lucy's testimony would be made. The only condition was we provide full disclosure, we felt maybe it was best not to interrogate him."

"30 minutes after we dropped him off? That's impossible!" Sarah shouted.

Kase replied, "We thought the same thing, and unfortunately that's not a hunch the CIA is going to talk to the FBI about; when it could have been one of you who led his embassy directly to our front door."

Cynthia squinted, "Are you saying there was a point in time where we were under investigation?"

"Not you," Kase replied. "Look guys, you don't get a man like Frank Fregoso walking into your safe house every day. He's the type of man that makes everybody a suspect and could rain down hell on anyone not on his side."

***

Samuel was escorted to the International Conference Room at MI-6 headquarters, in London, where he waited over an hour for the door to reopen.

"Hello Samuel, sorry about the wait, hope you're not bent with me."

Samuel smiled, "Cole, I know you're a busy man, thanks for seeing me."

SAS Chief Cole James replied, "They told me you made reservations to refuel with our air space and as much as I enjoy the company of a battle zone brother, something told me you were not here for tea. Now what brings you across the pond mate?"

Jeffries started, "Cole, can you tell me why no information was shared with your allies about Aiden Gina and Russia's new affair?"

"Assistant director Samuel Jeffries, I can tell you that there has been no information that requires attention on American soil, hidden from any of our allies by British Intelligence." Cole sat straight faced.

Samuel's smile faded as he realized that his obsession with Snitch had caused him to insult an old friend. "Thanks Cole. I just- I'm dealing with more political red tape then normal and it may be getting the best of me."

"Very well. What else may I help you with Samuel?"

"I'd like to run Frank Fregoso's last words through your linguists and see if they can determine what he said."

The glow left Cole's enthusiastic eyes as he replied, "Samuel I won't be able to do that."

"Won't or can't Cole? Because as the SAS Chief, it seems like you have all the ability to accomplish this request."

"Both Samuel!"

"Both, Cole! Really? Without even hesitation? You're telling me that Queen and Country are in bed with the Fregoso organization? These common criminals! These thugs in Armani suits."

"Don't be such a prig Samuel." Cole said, "Yes, we are friends, even allies but we don't hold the same belief in the accusations America used to kill Frank Fregoso."

Samuel yelled, "I didn't have Frank killed Cole! We fought side by side in the Gulf- some gnarly missions that nobody talks about and we did it to ensure that damn thing was put to rest properly. As a friend, having admired your rise to Chief and used your words of encouragement, please tell me we see eye to eye on this issue?"

"Samuel if you truly value my friendship, entertain me for a moment."

"For God's sake, Cole. The Fregoso organization is the number one arms dealer to the entire world, we're talking wars and innocent lives!"

Unfazed with Samuel's interruption Cole Continued, "Samuel we have indeed fought side by side on very dark missions, and were highly successful as allies. AD Jeffries, to think that we fought alone would be naïve-there were others with us. There was intel, favors asked and given and it was all things that helped defend our countries. Samuel, one of those allies that allowed both of us to navigate successfully was Portugal. As an American I don't expect your history books to include this, but I do expect you to understand what your academia refers to as the longest standing treaty between two countries. An agreement between countries making them our allies-our friends, Britain and Portugal made that agreement in 1376. What's most important for you to know is at the time that friendship was established your ancestors were simply Brits, and The Fregoso name is on that treaty Samuel. Yes, we have fought side by side- Britain and America, and that means as a Brit I was allies with the number two arms distributor to the world. Now before you allow your anger to out-grow your logic, ask yourself, where must the number two distributor of arms buy directly from?"

Samuel sat down hard on Cole's desk and asked, "What else Cole?"

"Samuel, when you get home check your history books, figure out how a bombing in paradise allows your country to fast- track nuclear fusion by six years and bring an end to the war with two bangs. You would be hard pressed not to find The Fregoso family name blacked out in your CIA's files which means that if we are in bed with him, there's American knickers in Frank's closet as well." Cole looked at his friend, "Samuel allow a friend to give you this advice, if you are traveling to a land where your credentials are meaningless, you're on vacation. That said, when you're in Portugal enjoy your vacation because if you are still content on chasing Frank Fregoso, you're going to his home. The only question that must be answered is are you going there to enforce American justice or to apologize to a nation for your part in the fall of their king?"

Cole extended his hand. Samuel holding onto a newfound truth-gripped his friend's hand, stood, and embraced him. "Thank you, Cole. Thank you for your honesty, I wish I had an answer for you."

"Samuel, Frank's death has brought the same passion and sense of duty to the forefront for all of us. Because of that we all must find a way to ground ourselves. In doing so remember that if you find yourself chasing the men who betrayed the king, you have sided your allegiance to His Majesty's court. Try to enjoy Portugal, Samuel."

"People keep telling me that." He replied.

"Listening would behoove you. Safe travels my friend."

Chapter 17

Samuel checked into his hotel in Lisbon, dropped his luggage and decided to go down to the bar for some assistance in digesting the information Cole provided. He forced a smile to the bartender as she smiled at him remarkably.

"Hello, I'll take an old fashioned please."

Samuel quickly dropped his head lost in thought. She bent slightly to allow her honey brown eyes to find his and smiled big, then asked, "An American old fashion or a Portuguese old fashion?"

Samuel- forgetting almost everything on his mind when her eyes found his, straightened his back and took in the entirety of her beauty, "There's a Portuguese old fashion?"

Her eyes sparkled as she bounced with excitement, "Of course! I'll make it for you and if you don't like it, it's on me."

"Thank you."

"Tudo bem."

Unable to control his smile, he questioned, "What did you say?"

She replied, "Tudo bem, it's like saying it's all good."

She turned and walked out of the bar flashing her beautiful olive skin and curves of her back through the crop top hiding behind her apron. Samuel watched the corner of the bar anxiously until he saw her lovely silhouette return a few minutes later with two dark red drinks in jars.

"Am I getting two?"

"No, but I'm from the west coast and we never allow guest to drink alone- it's just not polite."

She rose her drink, "Here's to your first Portuguese old fashion."

Samuel tapped her glass and took a sip out of the old Mason jar.

"This is amazing." He said surprised.

"Oh, you like it?" she smiled again.

"It's my new favorite drink." Samuel laughed. He introduced himself, "I'm Samuel."

"Gabbi." She replied.

"Funny, you don't look like a Gabbi, nor sound like a west coast girl."

She laughed, "That's because you still believe that California is the west coast but centuries before you discovered gold, Portugal was and will always be the true west coast. It's ok, your American eyes will adjust." She winked.

"That obvious?" He chuckled.

"Yes, but in the best way imaginable." She took another sip.

"So, what's in this Portuguese old fashion, Gabbi?"

The intenseness of her eyes sparkled as she held Samuel's gaze, "Imagine a bottle of wine allowed to reduce slowly to just a glass full of nectar, composed of all the beautiful grapes that gave their lives to create its genetic greatness. Pour that over a small frozen pyramid comprised of orange, lemon, and lime slices and top it with chopped iced-mint leaves and raw cane sugar. Then you add a bartender who understands that tradition is more important than time, until it is muddled exactly right; add one shot of the original wine and smile as you watch Portugal brighten up your heart as you drink."

"It's delicious."

"Obrigada," She smiled.

"That's one I do know, and you're very welcome Gabbi. Would I be breaking any tradition if I took this drink up to my room to retire for the evening?"

She flashed a smile, "That's what it's meant to do Samuel, allow one to retire for the night in complete tranquility. Enjoy Lisbon, goodnight."

That morning, Samuel hit Lisbon and the surrounding areas, walking through the streets and talking to everyone he could-but nothing, no one knew the phrase or understood the language. He continued his excursions for five days straight and extended his search throughout the cities within comfortable driving distance but the only thing he found was a reasonable car service, and a delightful Portuguese old fashion- ready to order when he returned to his hotel. Exhausted in the middle of yet another strange downtown area, Samuel called for a ride back to the hotel. In an act of desperation he asked his driver if he knew the phrase, pushing play on the recorder.

The driver looked in the review mirror, "That's not a language spoken here."

"You said here, you didn't say Portugal." Samuel shot back.

"Correct," The driver responded. "it's a country dialect, a lot further North- way North, long time from now. But if you're paying, I could take you there in the morning. We'd have to get up early."

Samuel's eyes got big, "That'd be amazing! Hey, thank you, I mean, Obrigado." He said when the driver dropped him back at the hotel. Samuel's enthusiasm about the next morning's potential soon turned to disappointment as he headed towards the elevator, giving the bar one last look back, hoping for her smiling face. Not finding her he turned and there she was-smiling in a cute dress and coat holding two mason jars.

"Someone order two old fashions again?" He asked, smiling like a teenage boy.

"No, silly, I saw you when you walked in. You had those same tired eyes you've had all week so I took it upon myself to bring drinks to you- instead of the bar stool."

"You're very observant for a bartender." Samuel joked.

"I'm a writer, I just bartend for the story's. I like to collect them and bartending is the perfect way to do it." Gabbi smiled.

"So what kind of story am I?"

She looked at him squinting, "I don't know but I'll tell you this, for a man who's been out all over Lisbon you're not happy. It's such a beautiful place, so before you go to bed tonight, you're going to see Lisbon the right way.

"What about our drinks?"

"This is not America, we're bringing them with us." She laughed as they walked out of the hotel.

They spent the night jumping on and off the tramway to refill their jars and grab delicious tapas. Of course, hearing Gabbi give a seductively intellectual history lesson on the architecture of the storefronts along the route was Samuel's favorite part of the evening. It was close to midnight when they got back and she grabbed his empty glass.

"I need to return these to the bar, it was a wonderful evening, I hope you rest well Samuel."

She stood tall on her tiptoes and kissed him gently on the cheek.

"Chao!"

She was halfway to the bar when his brain alerted him that the kiss was over and the polite thing to do in this moment is to reply, "Chao!"

***

The hard ring of the hotel phone rattled Samuel to the side of the bed. "Sir it is currently 5:00 AM and you have a car waiting for you." He heard the hotel Concierge say softly.

Samuel watched the sunrise come up on the Portugal countryside as they drove. The young man broke the silence pointing to the kilometers of farmland.

"Those are two of the finest wineries throughout the countryside."

Awestruck by the scenery Samuel replied, "It's amazing! You grew up with this scenery as your back yard?"

"Yes sir, I've actually eaten grapes off those vines as my mom shopped for wine. My name is Ontario and yours?"

"I'm Samuel. Thank you for doing this. You never actually said how much this trip was going to cost me."

The young man smiled, "You look to me like a good man, I believe you will pay me what you deem the trip worth."

"Does everyone in this country wake on the good side of the bed?" Sam asked with a smirk.

Ontario pointed to the west, showing Samuel the ocean coming around the bend of the road as it curved deep into northern Portugal and he chuckled, "There's a bad side of the bed?"

Samuel had no words for the young man's optimism. He sat back enjoying the view as the tall cliffs stood strong at the mercy of the intoxicating Atlantic Ocean. Soon Samuel found his gaze locked on a large sailboat effortlessly gliding up the coastline. He watched the captain maneuvering the vessel as he controlled ropes and sails like a conductor would an orchestra, he was mesmerized. After forty-five minutes Ontario said, "I hate to disturb you Samuel, but we are just outside of town."

Samuel quickly snapped out of it, "He makes those rough seas look powerless against that sailboat. How difficult is it to sail those seas?"

"It takes a captain with extraordinary focus and an impeccable ability to predetermine Mother Nature's next move." Ontario advised.

Samuel chuckled, "I'll stick with diesel and a navigation system that doesn't require me to see the future."

They made their way into the small town and it was breathtaking; a small assortment of 17th century aristocratic architecture that opened to a small downtown area with a historical castle standing center stage in the horizon. It over-looked the town like a large guardian angel standing post.

Ontario told Samuel, "I'll park by the pharmacy and wait for you."

Samuel spent two hours struggling to get any of the women in town to acknowledge his existence and the only man he could find was a Lisbon delivery driver. He walked back to the car feeling a little defeated. Ontario looked at him, "Any luck Samuel?"

He shook his head, "Nothing, and hardly any men in this town my friend, I'm afraid I've wasted both our time today."

Ontario gave him a side smile, "Never a waste of time Samuel, think of how much of Portugal you have been able to breathe in; and as for the men in this village, they are probably at the pub drinking."

Samuel looked at his watch. "It's not even 11am."

Ontario laughed, "It's always a good time for a drink. You look like you could use one, we'll have one together."

Samuel shrugged his shoulders as he got back in the car.

They drove through the center of town to its northernmost point just on the other side of the road leading up to the Castle. To the right sat an old tavern, they walked into the bar and saw thirty to forty men-all talking and laughing. Samuel feeling incredibly comfortable made his way to the bar.

"Bourbon on the rocks please."

"Yes Sir," the bartender said quickly then handed Samuel a glass of red wine. Samuel looked at the man, "Excuse me, I didn't order the wine."

The man smiled, "I'm aware sir, but Frank Fregoso would want you to drink a wine that was made under the care and love of his family."

Samuel's blood ran cold as he noticed every man in the bar standing still. The old man sitting on the barstool beside him turned to address him, "Assistant director Samuel Jeffries, if it's not the wine that you are looking for then what is it?"

Samuel turned to the old man noticing that none of the men had moved a muscle, "I can't be bought, I don't do favors, and there are people you don't want to piss off by not allowing me to walk out of this tavern sir."

The old man smiled, "Assistant director, the wine was brought to you out of respect for what you're doing."

Samuel cut him off. "For what I'm doing?"

"Yes! You are doing everything in your power to ensure that an old man did not die in vain- which is what we all want in this family; so, we raise our glass to you-the American hero that has chosen to seek justice for Frank Fregoso."

Samuel, hearing the reality of his job for the first time, felt at ease.

The man sitting next to him smiled, "Please, raise your glass for a toast to Frank Fregoso and in this jubilation may you find the words you have been seeking for so many years now."

Samuel raised his glass as the entire pub toasted and they spoke in unison the phrase from Samuel's recorder.

The old man tapped Samuel's and said, "Love is loyalty." And they drank their wine.

"Now, Assistant director Jeffries, you are a long way from Lisbon but there is a train that runs nonstop that will allow you to go back to your hotel faster and with views worth being still for. Would you care to walk with me?"

Samuel got up and as they walked out of the back of the pub he saw a beautiful train station nestled in the shadows of the castle. A luxury private car sitting securely between two blue steel 6000 horsepower, road switcher diesel electric locomotives.

"Not a very busy station." Samuel observed.

"The train is always on time."

"Ah, my driver!" Samuel snapped as he remembered his unpaid debt.

"My son will understand why he didn't drive you back to Lisbon, and it would be very late for him to get back after driving you home."

"Your son? Who are you?"

They stepped on the train and the doors closed.

The man smiled at him again, "My name is Ontario Fregoso the 17th. This is the home of my family-the original home of Francisco Fregoso the 1st, the father of this family many centuries ago, everything you see in between here and the vineyards is Fregoso family land."

Samuel interrupted, "What does the phrase love is loyalty mean?"

Ontario looked into Samuel's eyes, "It means that justice and the judgment of others should be based on love, it's the understanding that above our own will love must come first."

"How do you know my name?" Samuel asked.

"You're the agent that arrested Frank-my brother. We have watched you to see if you are truly the good man Frank believed you to be." Ontario said with a smile.

Samuel shook his head. "I'm guessing if I have any more questions, you're not giving?"

The man shook his head, "That's not what you came here for. You've already received that my friend, and now, it's a matter of what you do with it. There's no one in this country who has an ill will towards Frank Fregoso, so if you're looking for answers to whom would have done such a thing to my brother, you won't find them here. What you will find are 15-thousand men spread across the globe who all share the same last name. Men who have decided to live a life of loyalty and raise families and kingdoms across the world in honor of Francisco Fregoso the 1st."

The old man stopped. "It's not quite dinnertime in Lisbon, don't leave before you appreciate it."

The train came to a stop at the station in Lisbon.

"Thank you, Ontario," Samuel said as he stepped off the train.

He smiled, "You're welcome, Assistant director Jeffries. I wish you good fortune in your quest for American justice."

The doors closed as the train headed back North. Samuel walked slowly down the streets of Lisbon, back to the hotel locked in the mystery that is Frank Fregoso, the Fregoso family, and 15 thousand men that were potentially as powerful and influential as Frank; it was bigger than he could embrace.

Chapter 18

He smiled when he saw her sitting at the tables outside the hotel restaurant.

"Did I miss dinner?"

"Oh no one misses a Lisbon full moon, with appetizers and wine." Gabbi winked.

"Room for one more?" He smiled at her his eyes sparkling in the moonlight.

Her smile deepened, "Of course stranger, there's always room for one more." She winked.

He took the seat, "Thank you- I mean Obrigado. What's on the menu?"

Gabbi waived at the waiter, "I'll double what I ordered trust me you will love it!"

Samuel shook his head in awe, "You almost make life feel too simple."

She stared back raising her eyebrow, "Or maybe you make it too complicated?"

They both laughed as the waiter came by and she updated the order.

Samuel was finding it hard to keep the smile off his face, he looked across the table and could finally understand how beautiful Portugal really was. "When I was in the military, I use to tell myself during the moonlight beach drops that one day I would take the time to appreciate the waves crashing against the shore in the moonlight instead of just using it to camouflage a mission. I know there are waves here and a shoreline but I have no clue how to get there."

Gabbi grabbed his hand and smirked, "Drinks to go again!"

The two sat on the top of the cliffs watching the waves kiss the shore under a blanket of stars. Samuel wrapped his arm around her, "I think I came to Portugal for the wrong reasons."

She leaned her head on his chest and wrapped her arms around him tightly, "Or it just took you longer to find the right reason."

He kissed the top of her head securing his other arm around her.

"You know they call you a real hero in Portugal. They say you were tricked into the side of those evil men plotting against the King but because you are a true hero, you saw through the lies and pledge to help bring justice to those who were disloyal."

Samuel squinted, curling the strong wrinkles in his hand until his knuckles gave way to the bursts of battle corn popping. He leaned his cheek to her head and confessed, "A different me wanted him locked away forever for acts I couldn't prove, I couldn't separate the man from his sins and I didn't want to see that it was him doing everything in his power to love his family and those that loved him. I've always found being a warrior is easier if the enemy is vile with no redeeming qualities. I've never once in my career behind the battle lines-or the badge, felt that I have wronged a man until now. Gabbi I'm responsible for making things right and how I got here doesn't matter."

Gabriela rose her beautiful brown eyes to meet Samuel's, "My love, it is the fall that brings the hero out of humanity. The desire to pledge your loyalty to a King that has only been found guilty of loving his kingdom is what makes you the hero the Portuguese cheer about. We all must walk through our past as historians gathering facts." She paused and touched her lips to Samuel's. The exchange of electrons surged through his heart as Gabbi continued.

"The decisions you made based on the facts that you were presented does not define the man that you are Samuel. Hero's must battle through life's challenges like all of us, but you have chosen to provide justice for your country and that is why you are a hero."

Chapter 19

Kevin flashed his badge and started to ask the wrong people some very uncomfortable questions in a of couple underground establishments-it didn't take senior Agent Goodson long to push the right buttons in Chicago. The underground did what it does best and within days he had a confidential informant: J. Collins- a controlling partner in the Canadian cartel reached out to him. He provided Kevin with an encrypted flash-drive he kept from a prior arrangement with Aiden Gina. Collins acknowledged the pressure coming from the FBI to anyone tied to the Fregoso organization and presumed he should be worried and decided to cooperate.

With Samuel out of the country Kevin had been working directly with Director Murphy and once he had the drive in his possession he called the Director, "Murphy I've got something and it could be huge. Collins gave me a flash drive from Panama, it's supposed to have intel on Gina's movement since Frank hid him away."

Director Murphy ferruled his brow straining at the thought of Collins surrendering the flash to agent Goodson and shouted, "Kevin don't plug it in! Send it directly to me and find Collins. If this is an agreement between him and Aiden Gina he's not giving it up that easily unless it's just the tip of the iceberg. Kevin he knows more, make him talk- I don't care how. Find out who sent him to you."

***

The once corporative Chicago underground all but shut down when it came to tracking down Collins. He had all but disappeared. Kevin and

Murphy where able to discover Collins had his yacht at the Burnham Harbor and once they ascertained the dock number his vessel was assigned, Kevin went to investigate.

The leaves rustled past his feet as he made his way through the pedestrian track to see the waterfront. The midnight sapphire waters of Lake Michigan spread in all directions from the harbor and his eyes took in the sea of docked vessels that ranged from small dinghies to multi million dollar yachts. Kevin could hear the rhythmic chatter of the hundreds of rigging lines and pulleys as his feet left the concrete and stepped onto the wooden planks of the harbor entrance. He waited patiently for Chicago PD to pass him the security codes for the private docks and

moved in through the main entrance. Collins' boat would be on the 3rd dock. He swiftly made it down to the vessel and climbed onto the yacht-the interior lights were on. Kevin knocked on the door announcing himself, "Hello?" He walked down into the galley and saw Collins sitting, bent over the dining table with a gunshot wound to the head. Kevin reached for the man's hand as he called into Chicago PD.

"This is Special Agent Goodson, I need an ambulance to the Burnham Harbor now. I've got a man with a gunshot wound to the head." He whispered to the lieutenant, "Be advised, possible assailant on premises."

Collins's hand was still warm and his fingers bendable. Kevin bolted to the helm and grabbed the spotters binoculars and started to survey the four block bayside entertainment center.

His 911 call immediately sent notification to Director Murphy and he placed a call to mobilize Illinois FBI helicopter man-hunt units.

Kevin continued to look across the harbor scanning each deck for movement. It was huge though, each of the 50 docks holding 25 vessels. He scanned each row and his eyes caught a man walking pass dock 15 in a suit. He dropped the binoculars and ran to the main walkway. He was gone- nowhere to be seen. Kevin knew that the man had to have gone down a dock row so he ran full speed to the dock he spotted him at. He walked down the dock and gently climbed the larger vessels to inspect but saw nothing. He quickly returned to the main walk and over to dock row 16. Fearing that the suited man might have moved further down the docks, Kevin climbed the large sailboat in front of him and spotted the man on dock row 21, standing past the third boat looking up at the full moon over the lake. Kevin squeezed the rigging tight as he climbed down from the boat calmly, his heart pounded as his years of tactical trading steadied his movements to the dock row towards the man whom was back on the move. Snitch walked unhurried around the bend on the deck and Kevin acted. His feet bolted to the curve of row 21 and sprung at Snitch making contact in the center of his back. He locked his clench as the two men plummeted towards the deck. The jolt threw Snitch's head backwards and activated his unconscious cognitive survival instincts. He quickly put out his hands bringing both agent Goodson's force and the two of them to a halt before his chest hit the wooden planks of the deck. An abrupt stop happened as Kevin felt the man's body twisting in his arms, Snitch landed an elbow directly to Kevin's right temple and his hands released as Snitch continued to twist switching their positions. Kevin's chest was pinned directly to the deck and Snitch interlocked his left arm and grabbed the base of his neck. He secured Kevin's left arm to his body but instinctually, Kevin protected the side of his head realizing he had been immobilized. Snitch planted his knees into the Sr Agent's hamstring and used the grasp on the back of Kevin's neck to apply optimal force onto his body. Then Snitch began to land brutal punches to his rib cage and kidneys. Kevin struggled with the urge to protect his abdomen as Snitch's blows fractured his ribs. Snitch grabbed Kevin's right arm, braced it and locked it against the agent's head then used the leverage to raise his knee into Kevin's side crushing the 4th and 5th ribs. The hit sent shockwaves through Kevin's body. Snitch released his right arm and reared his hand back to land another hit giving Kevin no choice but to protect himself and pull all his might into trying to push the man off his back. In doing so agent Goodson allowed Snitch to swing his arm underneath his head and wrap and twist with him, securely clinching Kevin's neck. Kevin knew immediately as both their body's contorted, and the agent found himself on top of his assailant's chest with his oxygen being restricted, it was a matter of moments before his consciousness would be lost. Snitch locked his ankles around Kevin's legs immobilizing the agent and as he began to loose consciousness both men heard the faint sound of sirens blaring behind Soldier Field. Snitch used Kevin's legs as leverage and squeezed tightly and locked his grip harder around the agents throat. Sr agent Goodson was helpless as Snitch looked over his shoulder into Lake Michigan to see the lights of the helicopters and aquatic units heading towards the harbor. Satisfied that Goodson was completely unconscious he released his legs and rose both the men never releasing Kevin's choke. After a few more seconds Snitch slowly put him down to the left then sat on the side of the dock beside the large sailboat Sr agent Goodson lay unconscious behind. He buttoned his jacket and gently lowered himself into the harbor water.

The FBI and Chicago police breached Collins' yacht to find the dead man and as they began to search the FBI halo radioed in, "Harbor we have a twin unit escorting coastguard to confine all boats to the harbor." The halo spotter interrupted communications as he locked his spot light on Kevin's body, "Harbor, we have a man down 75 yards-dock 21!"

The vibration of his phone between him and the deck along with the commotion of boats and helicopters brought St. Agent Goodson back to consciousness. Kevin reached up to cover his face from the halo lights then reached in his pocket and waved his badge. Kevin grabbed his phone it was Murphy.

Director Murphy sat down giving his carpet a break from the pacing when Sr agent Goodson answered the line. "Kevin are you injured?"

Kevin stood up looking around the harbor at all the commotion, "He got away. Murphy it was snitch-he's gone! How far out were Chicago PD? There's no way he made it pass that damn stadium. He killed Collins, he's got to be here. Murphy it was him!"

"Kevin let them check you out and assess the situation it was 17 minutes between your 911 call and the halo locating you, make sure you're okay."

"Yes Sir." Kevin agreed. "The team's headed his way."

"Senior Goodson, are you okay?" The Chicago swat captain yelled.

Kevin waved his arms- lowering their sense of urgency, "I'm Fine, but he's here- our assailant could still be on premises."

"Sir, the ground units have dogs at the stadium and shipping warehouse and we have cleared 20 percent of the boats in the harbor."

Kevin looked at the distance from the docks to any main building, "He's not at the stadium! He's here! I heard the ground units coming in as we fought."

"Sir, we have units checking every boat in the harbor-"

"How long is that going take?" Kevin cut him off.

"Hours."

"We don't have hours!" He shouted.

Sr agent Goodson took a moment to clear his head and took a deep breath, "He didn't leave the harbor on a boat, he's too smart to not know we would check every vessel."

"If he didn't sir, he's hiding in a boat and we have every one of them in the harbor secure- it will just be a matter of time until we find him."

Kevin looked at the scattering of vessels outside of the harbor their stern lights dotting the Lake Michigan waters. He gently held the ice pack to his temple and ask the Chicago SWAT captain, "What about those, what if he made it outside of the harbor?"

The captain looked out towards the river mouth, "If he made it out of the harbor he could be anywhere between here and the 31st St Pier. That gives him access to all of Lake Michigan and the entire Chicago River."

It was after 2:00 in the morning when the FBI and Chicago PD finished searching all the vessels inside of Burnham Harbor. Kevin sat disappointed knowing that the vital minutes he laid unconscious allowed Snitch to slip away.

Chapter 20

Samuel sat in his office with Senior Agent Goodson staring at the dark navy bruising screaming for attention on Kevin's light brown skin. Samuel's chest released a strong gust of air, "Kevin, you don't owe anyone more than the Chicago case file. You don't have to tell the team anything you don't want to tell them about the situation at the harbor. Murphy's working on that flash drive and should have it unlocked with in the hour."

Kevin rubbed his hands against his pants, squeezed his thigh and straitened his back, "Thank you. We have all found our way into discoveries over the last two weeks and Chicago is part of it once we crack that drive we can pin Gina down. They need to know that this guy is prepared-he's not jumping without a net. He's got a back up for his back up."

Samuel's forehead wrinkled as he evaluated his agent's response, "Kevin I'm fine with taking lead in there but I need you to tell me if you think Snitch was trying to kill you?"

Sr agent Goodson's voice flared confidence, "No! He wasn't expecting me but he was prepared for guest. If he wanted me dead he would not have opted for sleep."

The agent's eyes were focused on Samuel telling him he was ready. The two walked down the hall to join the rest of the team in the huddle room and everyone sat quiet for a moment taken aback by Kevin's wounds. He immediately addressed the team saying, "I'll take lead on this one. I have information from Chicago being worked on but most importantly, I had my hands on Snitch."

Kevin curled both fist as the intensity in the huddle room began to brew. "I didn't see his face. He put a bullet in my CI, Collins and I tracked him to the docks. I was this close,"

He rose his hand allowing 3 cm to between his thumb and index finger. "but he's strong. Not-"

"Goodson you survived to tell the story!" Charles interrupted. The thoughts of surviving hand to hand combat with the enemy erupted in him and he couldn't contain it. "He got the best of you, this time but next time we get him. It's a damn good thing you got fight in you."

Kevin smiled and scratched the nape of his neck, "No Charles he is fucking strong. I was going full speed and perfect form tackled him from behind. He caught both of us on that deck with my momentum! My hands locked around his abdomen and never hit the ground. He caught us and immediately countered with a deafening twisting elbow to my temple. It was less than two seconds from me with the upper hand to him locking me in a rear naked choke-I was done. Next thing I know, I'm surrounded by FBI and tactical units. Snitch disappeared- we checked every boat in the harbor but he was gone. Like smoke through a keyhole."

Sarah smiled, "Bruised or not it great to see you Kevin. Whatever is on that drive was worth Aiden Gina killing for-what's our ETA?"

"Murphy is going to send it directly to me once it's unlocked." Agent Goodson stroked his goatee sitting down with a smile, "Look guys I'm okay. I may be the only one that took a beating on vacation but I'm not the only one here who has made discoveries and right now my discovery is waiting on our tech team to work their magic."

Charles immediately spoke up, "Okay then allow me to hand this over to Special Agent Cynthia Prince, our tree-hugging agent of the year!"

Cynthia looked at Kevin's large smile and bruised knuckles, "I'll make this quick because it's going to create more questions then answers but it will shed light on the scope of Gina's influence. We went back to the facility in Colorado and discovered two important things: One, Snitch stayed on premises-just inside the tree line the entire Fregoso stay. The most important, and perhaps hardest to digest is the fact that Frank's people knew the facility where he was being detained-not just the address. They called the CIA safe house directly within 30 minutes of you guys dropping Frank."

Samuel stood up and looked down the hall towards Deputy Director Tanner's office, "Love is loyalty. That's what Frank said the morning of his death to his daily embassy call. Now that we know the Portugal embassy knew we were taking Frank to a CIA site they had on speed dial, we can look back and see clearly. Team we missed something major when we picked Frank up in 2016. We didn't account for the span of Frank's control and we didn't think a family member with all of Frank's influence could have been in that hospital and followed us out. I met some of Frank's brethren in an entire city of his lineage. They were smart and pleasant yet I could tell that they may all have some measurement of power in this world."

Kevin interrupted, "You said they, how many of them are there?"

"There are 15,000 Fregoso men." Samuel sat down. "They all speak a documented language the Portuguese call Mardenesse, and unless a Fregoso male taught you the language you will never learn it. Francisco Fregoso the 1st, one of the founding fathers of modern Portugal established it teaching it to only his boys in 1245 AD. Now 15,000 men like Frank that don't exist in any country's files- yet are in every country's history are all diligently doing some kind of knowledge transfer to the next generation. Guys the Fregoso Family does not seem to be connected to Frank's organization but they have the power to exact vengeance, and I sense if we don't catch Snitch first they will kill him eventually. Right now a brilliant Colorado find nor my Portugal stumbles tell me what just happened on your laptop to cause that smile Kevin."

Kevin loaded the main screen with a passage document from the Panama Canal, "We got Gina's Atlantic passage route for the past seven years- all signed off by one customs agent. My CI was worried that the new King Pin would flex his muscles and after a few of his men found their asses locked up in Chicago's finest jail cells he thought it smart to talk. This sequence number in place of the agent's name is assigned by the CIA. It's the only sequence number assigned to 100% of Gina's pass-throughs."

All of a sudden Charles popped up and ran out of the room, you could hear him screaming down the hallway, "Tanner!"

John Tanner stepped out of his office, "A quarter of professionalism please, Special Agent Stevens."

"Yes Sir. Sequence numbers for customs agent?"

"Sequence numbers are employee numbers for customs agents, the sequence number correlates to an actual passport identification number. It's no algorithm, every third digit will become the identification number of your agent's passport."

"Tanner your ex-CIA traits worry me as a military man but you're damn useful."

Tanner heard him say as he ran back to the huddle room. He announced, "Run the sequence on the third number identification search in the passport records."

"Tanner told you that?" Kevin asked.

"He told me how they make sequence numbers for customs."

"Those guys are different types of secret agents," Kevin smiled. "What did we get?"

"Eduardo Gealina."

"How do we find him in Panama?"

"We don't, we watch and pray he shows up to work tomorrow." Charles looked at Kevin.

The phone rang, Samuel answered the speakerphone and the voice announced, "Sir, the US embassy in Brazil for you, it's been marked urgent."

"Send it through please."

A scared male voice with a strong Spanish accent frantically asked, "Hello?"

"Assistant Director Jeffries, Good morning may I ask to whom I'm speaking?"

"Eduardo Gealina, Sir. Please I need your help!"

The team moved quickly as they began to track the call.

"Stay calm young man I'm here to get you help," Samuel said as he pointed to Charles' laptop.

He muted the phone and pointed to Charles, "What did you find?"

"He's been tagged with possible ties to Frank Fregoso and all embassy files bookmark our office if detained. The trace is tracking a cell in Panama but we need to get him off that speakerphone to get a more accurate location. The embassy transfer is interfering and anyone could be listening."

Eduardo's voice broke in pleadings, "Please. Please, Sir. I'm in trouble, so much trouble. I need your help."

Samuel unmuted the line, "You're here with my team, I want you to write this number down and call me back immediately!"

"Yes sir!"

"Write this phone number down. 841 438 7575. You've called the right place. Do that now Eduardo!"

Samuel hung up the speakerphone and his cell began to vibrate immediately. "Eduardo where are you?"

"I'm headed to my home in Brazil."

"How long is it going to take you to get home?" Samuel asked.

"By the morning, on the train."

"We're going to get to Brazil and figure out a way to get you into the American Embassy where you will be safe, OK?"

"Yes Sir! Thank you! I know they are looking for me."

"How do you know that Eduardo?" Samuel asked, a little puzzled.

"The man I made the agreement with in Chicago called me and they killed him! Please sir I need your help! I don't want to die!"

"Eduardo you are going to be ok." Samuel comforted. "You're with the right side now, I need you to calm down and tell me exactly what happened. Who is the man in Chicago?"

"Jea Collins, Sir. His name was Jea Collins."

Kevin pointed to the screen as Eduardo continued, "He called me last night and said that I was not safe, that a Mr. Aiden Gina wanted me dead then he pleaded for his life as I heard gunfire."

"Eduardo what was the deal you made with Collins?"

"I'm so sorry! It was a lot of money and all I had to do was allow one private owner unrestricted canal passage. I don't want to die! They know where I work, Sir. I need your help."

"We are going to help you Eduardo but you are not going to be safe until you are out of Panama." Samuel reassured him.

"Yes sir, I'm on a train now. Please hurry."

"Eduardo you're doing the right thing. Put your phone down and don't draw attention to yourself." Samuel told him.

"I don't want any harm to come to my family sir."

"Eduardo no harm is going to come to your family. Does anybody else know about the deal you made with Collins?"

"No Sir."

"We're going to get you safe. What major city will you be closest to in Brazil?"

"Once home I'm a short train ride to Rio, Sir."

"You're safe now Eduardo, I'll talk to you soon young man."

"Thank you, Sir!"

"Take care, son." They heard the phone hang up.

Murphy stood in the door of the huddle room unnoticed by the team.

"I want all of you in Rio now! Get this guy back to FBI headquarters, he knows more than he's saying. Extract him. Don't ask permission- don't even check in with the local government. Get your team to Brazil, Samuel. I'll set up your satcoms and run point from my office."

The team was determined that grabbing Eduardo directly from the train station would be the safest way to ensure that there was no influence from any outside sources. They coordinated the metro station layout and optimal positioning then tried to get some sleep on the G6. They would have to go directly to the train station to set up surveillance cameras under the cover of darkness and learn the Rio train arrival patterns to successfully corral Eduardo.

***

Charles sat on the station platform with only three other passengers and intercomed in, "My platform is dead no way we do a night grab there are too many hiding places."

The team all concurred and set up surveillance on the arrival tracks for the afternoon schedule. Samuel's phone rang, "Eduardo, how are you doing Sir?"

"I feel sick but I will be better when I know my family is safe."

"You said you could get to Rio in the morning right?"

"Yes Sir, there's a train there and I can get into the station within two hours."

"That's what I want you to do tomorrow afternoon and we'll walk you through it. Eduardo I brought my entire team with me to make sure that you're safe, we're going to get you to the US Embassy and to America. Then you will be safe and your family will be out of harm's way."

"Yes Sir. Thank you, sir."

"Eduardo I want you to call me at 7:00 AM your time and we will discuss the train schedule."

"Yes Sir."

Samuel heard dial tone.

Samuel and Cynthia checked the train schedules and they all converged on the main platform.

"This place is a nightmare." Kevin ran his hands through his hair and shook his head, "It's got so much movement."

"If it's a nightmare for us, it's a nightmare for Gina's men too and we've got the element of surprise." Charles pointed out.

"Fair enough, so what's the plan?" Kevin asked.

Samuel and Sarah looked at each other.

"What are you thinking Montgomery?" Samuel asked.

Sarah spoke up, "There are only these two main tracks that run from his town, so if we put him on train 033 at 10:10 we will be on the main station platform for its arrival, that's the platform we want. Otherwise you'd have to cross tracks or stairs to get him to a car. There we can grab him immediately and go straight down the platform to the exit."

"Cynthia, Kevin, what about my eyes?" Samuel asked.

"We are live with Murphy now." Cynthia confirmed. "He will be able to watch our six and should be able to see all the other cars loading and offloading passengers, the entrance, and the overhead pedestrian bridge." The team double-checked the schedule and surveillance then hurried to the hotel to coordinate with Murphy.

"What do you see Murphy? Samuel asked.

"Oh my God this place is large. What track are we looking for?" Murphy looked at the multiple camera views.

"Looking to grab on the main platform directly at the stairs." Charles answered.

"Ok team, it looks like the third set of doors on car three stop directly at the snatch site with two pillars flanking either side, that's where the grab team should stake their claim. If you can cover the southern stairs there is no vantage point we won't have possession of."

"Copy." Everyone answered with agreement.

"Get some sleep ladies and gentlemen and be ready in the morning. We don't get gifts like Eduardo every day. Make this count!" Murphy told the group.

Chapter 21

The team arrived at the Metro station in Rio early that morning determined to identify every advantage point Aiden Gina might have in the hunt for Eduardo. They split up at the main station to ride on separate trains out of Rio to the substitution and back because it would be the only reconnaissance the team would have to rely on as they prepared to guide Eduardo into Rio.

Cynthia spoke gently into the communication earbud, "This place is amazing. I think If you pictured Frank Fregoso and his entire lineage you would see Rio de Janeiro. Portugal's influence is everywhere."

Sarah walked across the crowded pedestrian bridge with the hundreds of early raisers, "I'm in position M, ghost recon until I track you into the main station."

Charles was the first to the turn around and noticed the generic subway traffic. It was medium to light with men in leisure suits, couples causally chatting, and workers moving intentionally. The car was not as smooth as a New York subway but it served a purpose. Charles' car came to a halt at the station switch and the doors opened. A man standing with the crowd to board looked Charles directly in the eyes and pointed down to butt of his weapon made visible when Charles grabbed the metro train's stabilization bar as the car made its stop

Snitch made eye contact with agent Stevens and in Portuguese politely said, "My friend there is no need for a weapon you are a friend here in Rio."

Charles looked at him acknowledging that his that weapon was slightly exposed and dropped his hand, "I'm Sorry, I don't speak Portuguese."

"It's okay my friend," Snitch quickly replied placing his hands palms out, "no one here wants any trouble."

Charles nodded in acceptance and covered his weapon as Snitch stepped into the subway car and stood four feet behind him for three stops. Snitch exited within arm distance from Charles stepping out of the exit- opposite doors from where agent Stevens stood. He turned to Charles and smiled, "Have a good day my friend." Charles nodded and patiently waited to reunite with the rest of the team at the main station.

The 033 train to Rio was on time with Eduardo sitting in the seventh car as instructed. The team spent the morning hopping in and out of trains to the grand station testing communication lines and checking views with Murphy as the clouds began to burn away. Eduardo checked in two stops before the grand station.

Samuel answered, "Eduardo I want you to move to the fifth car now and wait there until you stop at the main station. Once the train comes to a complete stop walk at a nice pace to the third car, then exit immediately. There will be an American man and woman with FBI credentials there to grab you and bring you to me. I am driving you to the embassy myself."

"Thank you Mr. Jeffries."

"See you soon Eduardo. Stay calm you're with the good guys now." Samuel ended the call and addressed the team. "Charles, I want you and Cynthia on the traveler platform now and Kevin and Sarah to the stairs. We get one shot at this, I will signal the intercept and we will move off quickly. Team, once we have him I want you off those stairs and in the car. Murphy, what do you got?"

"Samuel we have a horrible glare after 45 degrees, the sun is shining directly into the station. Your top views are going to have to watch the pedestrian bridge."

"That's fine," Kevin answered quickly, "Sarah take the southern deck, I can watch the pedestrian bridge and see the middle platform with my back to the sun."

Eduardo called, "Mr. Jeffries Sir, the train is stopping."

"My team is on the platform waiting on you."

"Yes, Sir. Thank you." his voice shaky.

"Eduardo put your phone down to your side and just walk easily. The agents are going to grab you."

"Yes, Sir."

"Here we go team."

Murphy spoke, "I got him-blue jeans, black jacket."

"Kevin what can you see?" Samuel asked.

"I got the whole train, he's in car four now."

Charles and Cynthia both acknowledged visuals as they moved towards the train with the boarding crowd.

Murphy intercomed in, "He's at the doors!"

"Got him on the left." Cynthia confirmed as she moved within a few feet of him.

"Kevin, Sarah, get to the car now." Samuel ordered.

Charles reached for Eduardo's arm as Snitch's AX50 round caused a distinct percussion as it made contact with the concrete, echoing through the train station. Bystanders began to scream as Eduardo's body fell to the ground with fragments of his brain tissue sounding the panic alarm. Charles drew his weapon as Murphy shouted over the com, "Samuel get your men out of there now!"

Cynthia grabbed Charles's arm pulling his firearm down to his side, "Charles there's nothing we can do, holster the fucking gun!"

The team stood in the grand foyer of the American embassy as Charles broke the silence they had all shared the entire drive, "What the hell is really going on? Boss there was only one other person on this operation and it just happens to be the man that sent us to catch Frank in the beginning!"

Back home Samuel barged into Director Murphy's office closing the door behind him. "How the hell does that happen Jason? It was a 48-hour operation. Someone set us up! Someone in the FBI!"

Director Jason Murphy focused on Samuel's disappointment and not his accusations as he began to speak, "You're right Samuel you were set up. Someone gave detailed information to Snitch allowing him to be with you and your team every step of the way. He tapped your phone. We reconstructed the reverse link while your team was in the air, he initiated the virus and started the reverse-trace with Eduardo's phone. The theatrical death of Collins in Chicago kept Eduardo on the line long enough to lock the tracking and load the program. That means once you were on the phone more than three minutes the advanced trace had your conversations in real-time."

"How the hell does Gina have all our best tech?"

"The real question Samuel is how many small confrontations and phone calls with vital information did we lose before we bought the technology?"

"Jason, Snitch is moving around like he works for the American government and my team is just here to clean up his damn mess and accept his rewards."

"What are you saying Samuel?" Murphy asked, making eye contact.

"I'm asking what side you're on, Jason?"

"Samuel, I know you're frustrated so I'll answer that question not like your boss but like a man who has spent his life swimming through American politics and legal systems. I stand to put those that are bad true evildoers behind bars permanently. Samuel in this situation there is only one side to stand on and that's right beside you, that's where I stand."

"Thank you, Murphy I'm-"

Murphy put his hand up, "Samuel we both know there are two sides to those plaques hanging on the wall. The side everyone sees and the side that gets nailed to the wall. Shutting down the FBI's

Most Wanted list comes with honors and raises but our governing agencies are asking questions. Questions like, are we setting up Snitch to spike the volleyball or did we make up a red herring to get away with an FBI sanctioned extermination of the Fregoso Organization. Samuel, understand there will come a time when we will have to show something more than a sniper round to prove his existence."

Chapter 22

The spacious four-bedroom, two-story luxurious log cabin sat nestled in a two-acre grove surrounded by the trees of the Smoky Mountain range. On the back patio a CIA agent sat in a chair as a young woman walked out holding her coffee.

"The morning mist is beautiful here you can see all the animals come out to feed on the fresh grass." She sighed, holding her coffee with two hands looking out, the steam from the mug filling her nostrils with the coffee's aroma.

"How long do we have to live here?"

The agent gave a side smile, "We don't know. We do know that what you saw that night with the UN official and Aiden Gina was wrong and you shouldn't have been in that situation. The information that you have will send him away for a long time and you'll never have to worry about hiding in the mountains or have an armed stranger always by your side again."

"I don't know." She turned and looked at him leaning against the rail. "There's something comforting about having a personal security guard always beside me." She took a sip of her coffee and winked at the man. As he started to speak her hands involuntarily widened and her spine stiffened and her shoulders went back, dropping the coffee cup in front of her feet. The strong thud into the wooden back door of the cabin broke the agent's concentration as he jumped up from his chair drawing his weapon. He quickly glanced at the arrow stuck in the door slathered in blood. Her lifeless body fell to the patio floor as he jumped the railing and started running expeditiously straight to the tree line firing rapidly. He emptied an entire magazine running full speed and as he made his way close to the trees the shot hit him directly in the neck. His arms begin to fall to his side as the shadow carrying the crossbow holstered a small handgun. The agent hit the forest floor unable to move as the sedative raced through his blood and the shadow walked towards him. Snitch bent down and removed the agent's pen from his pocket and walked back into the woods.

Minutes later Director Arsenault head of the CIA called Director Murphy, "Murphy seems we have a situation."

"What type of situation could the CIA have that would require calling me?"

"We have a non- responsive agent after alerting a compromised asset in Tennessee."

"Seems to be a lot of that going around but I'm not exactly sure what that has to do with the FBI, Paul."

"Murphy both agent and asset were at John Tanner's cabin. I'm sending you the address now, the possible asset down was the only witness in the case of the UN versus Aiden Gina."

"Paul you owe me more than a favor for this. I'm sending Samuel's team and calling you back."

Director Murphy selected a new line and called Samuel's phone.

"Samuel you and your team need to get to Tennessee now. The address is on your phone- I'll brief you on the plane."

Director Murphy hung up the phone before Samuel could respond and walked into John Tanner's office. John Tanner hung up his phone as Director Murphy slammed his door. Tanner spoke immediately, "I take it by that look Jason you got a phone call from an old friend of both of ours?"

"I got a phone call from the head of the CIA- your old boss about an agent and an asset down at your cabin John. Why the hell are they at your cabin?"

Deputy Director Tanner straightened his back, "When I took this job I told you there's only one person who outranks you and if he needs CIA assistance, I'm CIA. Besides Murphy, we are all trying to accomplish the same thing."

"Really? What is that, John?"

"Director as your subordinate I apologize but as a subordinate yourself you understand sometimes orders don't get shared up the ladder."

"We are not done Tanner, this is not the last of this conversation John."

"Didn't expect it would be."

Murphy walked out slamming the door.

Samuel's team arrived at the cabin and were met by a team from the CIA. The section chief addressed Samuel, "The ground floor patio is the scene and the Agent assigned is in the kitchen ready to talk."

The team walked into the cabin, "Wow! I guess if you got to be in witness protection this is the spot, this place is posh." Kevin spoke out.

"Yeah, fancy as hell until you catch an arrow to the eyeball." Sarah's frustration coming out as sarcasm.

Samuel and the team stood in the kitchen with the section chief and the agent assigned to the cabin. He addressed the man, "Special agent, I need to know everything you know about this morning."

He looked at the section chief from the CIA and received a head nod. The agent took a drink from his mug, "Approximately 0800, I went out on the back patio for coffees and everything was normal. Deer going through the field, a light mist on the ground, and birds singing. The asset came out at 0817 and we made small talk- what to expect, timelines, things of that nature. As she turned away from the field an arrow entered the back of her head and exited her right orbital socket. It was actually the arrow hitting the wood on the door that I heard before noticing that she dropped her coffee mug. I coded in as I drew my weapon and returned fire as I crossed the field. As I reloaded something hit me in the neck and within one step, I felt my gun drop. My knees began to buckle and I saw the shadow of a man come out from behind a huge tree. He had a crossbow in his left hand and was holstering a weapon walking straight at me. That's when I felt my back hit the ground and I woke up to adrenaline being administered right there in the field."

Cynthia looked around at the team, "Sounds a lot like Orlando, Agent how long have you been assigned to this post?"

The agent looked over to see his section chief nodding his head in agreement, "In this house? Seven months Ma'am."

Samuel trying to control his rage, turned to the CIA station chief, "OK, its all yours to process. Team let's move out."

Chapter 23

Aiden Gina stood on the deck of his yacht smiling as he dialed out on his satellite phone. He heard the other line pick up, "You understand that there's going to be bloodshed in your house Tom? I don't care if it's some poor bastard that must take one on the chin or if you make your little bitch boy squeal. Just know for this to end correctly we have to set things right. Our alliance is only as strong as the secrets that we hold for each other and right now I am holding a killer of a secret Tom. Of course if you don't like my choices I wouldn't mind you being the sacrificial lamb. It's just a dollar figure to him so I suppose you should come up with a good plan and the money for the new target, agreed?"

He heard Tom take a deep breath, "Agreed."

"Oh, and Tom, if you ever hide another thing from me again it will be your pound of flesh I have him collect." Gina stated sternly and hung-up.

Chapter 24

Martin Groshki stood in the premier luxury box at Old Trafford Stadium cheering on Manchester United in a match versus New Castle, when his phone rang. A familiar voice came through the line when Martin greeted the caller, "Now that you've been back in the land of the living boss man, you know it's okay to take a plane from time to time."

Gina laughed, "It's been a long time traveling on Poseidon's grace my friend. I don't think I'll ever be home on land again, I've gotten used to all this water-it provides my soul peace."

"Maybe Frank knew you better than you knew yourself." Martin raised his fist in silent cheer as United stole the ball.

Aiden paused on the other end as the words took him to a time when things were much different. The feelings turned from joyous to sickening quickly and he replied, "It's time for Tom to pay for his part in the reorganization of my family. It's been a year since that lying bitch met her end yet I still feel the Americans stalking."

"How do you want to handle it?" He sat back in his chair enjoying his luxury suite. "Our year of total freedom could come to an end quickly if we kill him."

"He is currently untouchable but the American political system will force him to be exposed. We will wait for now but I'm going to head up the Hudson to remind our public officials in the United States that I'm the king now. Once they realize that not even their protectors are safe, they will understand that the bargain chips they believe they are holding have expired."

Groshki smiled as he stood back up putting his hand against the glass, "We have made a rich man out of a killer we have never met and you want to give him more work? How do you know he will take another job? Especially one that will exact the wrath of the world's biggest bully."

"He has an unhealthy sense of loyalty and who he kills doesn't bother him. He knows he is nothing more than a ghost story and that allows him to take contracts no other assassin would take."

"Then your next move here is lunch because I'm tired of helicopter trips over the ocean- makes me queasy." He said sarcastically.

"You always had a light stomach for such a tough guy, enjoy your football game. I'll see you in a couple of weeks."

He hung up the phone and continued yelling at the home team's umpire as the door to his luxury box opened gently.

Snitch walked directly behind Martin as he yelled at the glass after the third penalty was dished to his team. He was holding a one-inch thick, 3-foot long, industrial zip tie he had connected with the first eleven inches already through the tension box.

Snitch put the zip tie over Martin's head and around his neck. Using his left hand and knee, Snitch slammed Martin to the glass and pulled the zip tie to the tightest position allowed.

He took a step back as Martin spun himself around onto the glass. Unable to say a word he began to franticly reach for the tail of the zip tie terrified, he looked at Snitch.

Snitch looked into the dying man's soul and as Martin drove his nails beyond the surface of his torn flesh into the blood spewing muscle fibers of his neck in a failed attempt to loosen the snare. He said to him, "Today you die for your betrayal to Frank Fregoso."

Martin Groshki hit one knee no longer pulling at his neck as the zip tie began to exact Frank's silent vengeance. The finality of his demise set in as Martin's will surrendered to unconsciousness leaving his body lying on the floor dying. Snitch walked around to a small desk with stationery and pulled out the CIA agent's pen to write then walked out of the luxury box.

"Cole what's going on?" Samuel answered his ringing cell phone concerned.

"Samuel your phone number was left on a piece of stationery on a desk only two meters from the dead body of Martin Groshki."

"How did he die?"

"He was strangled with an industrial zip tie. The details are uploading to our Langley link. Samuel the killer used one of your Central Intelligence Agency pens to compose his note to you."

"Cole, it was him-it was Snitch!"

"We have a very dead, extremely dangerous man removed permanently from the world without any judicial barriers. I don't care who it was, he did us a favor."

"Yeah, we've had that talk. Once again thanks for the intel Cole."

Samuel walked out of his office coffee in hand and into the huddle room to greet the team, "Good afternoon, where is Cynthia?"

"She has been down in the video lab for hours, said she would be up once she finishes." Charles informed.

Samuel walked to the Fregoso organization chart and crossed out Martin Groshki's face, "I got a call from the Chief of the SAS, the Brits found Martin Groshki dead a few hours ago in a VIP suite at Old Trafford Stadium after the Manchester United soccer game."

Sr Agent Goodson sat reclined in his chair taken aback as Cynthia walked in the door beaming with excitement to see Martin's body load on the screen.

"They found Martin." Samuel told Cynthia making sure she was caught up.

Her eyes still beaming, she sat down- almost prancing in her seat, "How did he die?"

A one-inch zip tie secured tightly around his neck."

"Damn.He put up one hell of a fight." Charles blurted.

"That's all self-inflicted? There was no sign of a struggle. Snitch strangled him without a touch but was gracious enough to return the pen he stole from the cabin." Samuel changed the picture to show the piece of stationary with his cell number on it.

The team sat perplexed."What the hell just happened?" Kevin looked up at Samuel. "Who in the hell just jumped in the game?"

Cynthia began to talk but Samuel's cell phone rang, stopping her from answering Kevin.

Samuel's eyes dilated as his pulse quickened as he looked up from his phone, "It's coming from my office." He looked at the team, "Assistant Director Jeffries."

"I believe you call me Snitch," Said the man on the other end.

Samuel swallowed his heart as a silent rage began to brew inside. He frantically motioned to the team and covered the phone whispering, "It's him! It's Snitch!"

Snitch began to speak again, "Take your time Sam."

The team moved swiftly, Cynthia jumped up with Kevin and headed down the hall to the tech team while Charles and Sarah logged in to triangulate Snitch's location.

"It doesn't sound like you're happy with the name assigned to you?"

"Sam it's not about my happiness but if you have to call me something, give me a name- you can call me Frank."

"Oh, No, I don't think so." Samuel snapped.

"Sam indulge me for a moment if you will. Time is what you want in this situation."

"By all means." Samuel quipped.

"Obrigado. Sam, there is a rock formation called the Eye of Africa- it's breathtaking. It's believed that the King of the universe once used it to look upon his creation and those that are privileged enough to travel and see this gift of nature, must elevate high into the heavens. Without any written laws the structure requires all that partake in its divinity to see from a view they do not naturally pose. But Sam, you could grab all the men and women in all of your American agencies and drop them into the structure and no one would realize they were walking in the vision of the King. Allow your vision to see from a higher perspective than your justice system." Snitch finished then disconnected the line.

Samuel put his phone down and looked at Sarah and Charles, "He's gone!"

Cynthia and Kevin ran into the huddle room. Kevin asked, "Did we find his position?"

"That was him!" Charles raised his voice.

"What did he say? We couldn't hear in the tech room." Cynthia asked.

"He said there's a rock feature that you can see from space called the Eye of Africa, and that we or I would need to raise my vision higher than just our justice system to see clearly."

Samuel paused as the door opened, seeing the tech team with their heads down.

"What do we have?"

"We have nothing, Sir."

"What do you mean we have nothing? My phone is on one of our most advanced trace systems we have and he was on the phone well over three minutes."

"Sir, there's nothing." The agent shook his head.

"Sir, it says you called yourself from your office and said nothing for three minutes."

The techs walked out of the huddle room and everyone sat there stunned. Cynthia leaned in, "Sir, what else did he say?"

Samuel looked at her and refocused on Snitch's conversation, "He advised we could call him Frank, he knew we called him Snitch."

"Call him Frank," Sarah erupted. "Frank Fregoso? What an arrogant, narcissistic bastard. Frank Fregoso is not this violent, vile man like Brussia or Vosh. He operated a balanced organization; the damn thing is on tilt because he's gone."

Charles lost his temper and shouted, "Wow, he's fucking hacking our systems and he thinks somehow he deserves to take a dead man's honor!"

Cynthia was quiet, almost perplexed. "That's beyond bold." Kevin stood up from the table, "He displays a willingness to take credit for what a man has spent a lifetime building just because he was willing to kill him doesn't give him inheritance to Frank's Kingdom. He's crossed the line."

The team traded back and forth with Cynthia still quiet until Samuel stopped everyone, "Wait a minute, hold on. When I was in Portugal, they kept telling me Obrigado. Obrigado-it's Portuguese for thank you. A Fregoso man told me thank you for doing this investigation. We just spent thirty minutes defending Frank Fregoso, the man we were on fire to imprison almost four years ago. What if Snitch has been doing the same thing we're doing right now?"

"Exactly!" Cynthia shouted collecting everyone's attention. "Guys, Snitch is going to kill Aiden Gina and anyone that took willing participation in Frank's betrayal. Look at what I found in the archives."

She punched into her laptop, pulling up a three -framed sequence of stop-motion videos of Frank Fregoso in his cell.

"The middle picture is Frank's last chess game. As he waits for the opponent's last move running left and right are all of Franks chess games before that night. On all of these I've imposed three stars-running vertically, the lower star is the trajectory point in which Snitch's sniper round hit Frank in the chest. The second star is the position that Frank is looking at on every other chess match- except for the last one. And the third star is of course, the position that he's looking at during the last chess match. When I ran the analysis of all these there were two things in common: The first is that Frank was never looking at the moon, the moon was never at that angle any night that he played. The second is Frank's trajectory for every night of chess that he played for those three months. It's looking exactly at Snitches camp in the trees and it's only during the last game that he's looking up at the highest angle. They are playing chess together and the last night they played from Snitch's sniper nest up the mountain-not his base camp. He's playing chess with him and every night but the last night Frank started the chess game. On the last night the chess table is turned- Snitch is allowed the first move and he moves the king's pawn from E2 to E4 - the same pawn that was picked up off of Audrey's desk. Frank was in control of this entire thing he was teaching Snitch every strategy that was needed for him to learn. When I put up Frank's last moments on all three screens you'll see Frank smile as he receives Snitch's last move which is an unavoidable checkmate. He makes the last move, looks up at Snitch, smiles and lowers his King. As we watch this twenty times slower you can see Frank's hands hit the chest table, a tear leaves his eye and his pupils dilate. At this moment Frank Fregoso passed away and it's a full four frames later that Snitch fires his round into Frank's chest. In essence, starting a new game-his game. The game that Frank taught him, the game we are all somehow entrenched in. Snitch didn't kill Frank."

"Oh my God!" Kevin said knocking his chair down as he bolted to his feet.

Sarah looked at Samuel as he spoke up, "His hand never moved, he was dead before the bullet hit him, Snitch would have known that. Frank had moonlight shining directly on the chess table illuminating the chalkboard he was using to teach. Just like in fucking Rio de Janeiro-at the train track with Eduardo! Snitch used the sunlight to blind us and spotlight his target. The cameras couldn't see anything because there was a glare. Frank Fregoso didn't find a room to play chess by the moonlight, he found a room to teach his assassin how to draw out and punish everyone involved in the coup against him." He looked at Cynthia, "Great work! How did you know to look back at the first round?"

"There were a few things that made me question what was going on but when we were in Colorado, Charles said if Snitch wanted to stage an assault on that safe house he was at the perfect vantage point. That Frank chose the one cell that strategically put him in the perfect location to keep him safe from the sniper's nest. I added that to the information CIA Kase gave us about the Embassy call and I quickly realized Frank made the decision that saved our lives-along with every CIA agent working in that facility. He did that because it wasn't the FBI nor the CIA that set him up but he needed to know who. So I thought about Frank as if we placed him there, we would send our best out to communicate with him and if things went south protect him if we needed to breach. I believe Portugal or rather, the Fregoso family, sent their best out." Cynthia said confidently.

Samuel kept their attention after Cynthia paused, "Now it makes sense. Snitch said we could put all of our agents from all of the American agencies in that structure and not see what he can see from above."

"Then why not kill us? He could have taken us out at that train station." Sarah asked, her face ghost pale.

"Because Frank knew we were just doing our job- he greeted us in the foyer." Charles answered. "He even warned us before he said goodbye that day, remember? He said,*Just know not all sources of information, witnesses, and smiling faces are loyal good people. Sometimes loyalty shows its face in places you don't understand*"."

"What are we going to do?" Asked Cynthia.

"What can we do?" Kevin replied quickly.

Chapter 25

Aiden Gina's mega-yacht sat snuggled in the Champlain Lock leaving one dam to cross before his vessel would be in the Hudson River. He wanted to be close when his American partners felt the extent of his reach. He discussed the harbor master's protocol with his head of security. "Shane I've made arrangements for a meeting late tonight. He should be alone and I want him scanned and physically searched. If he's not alone or your search reveals any type of weapon put a bullet through his head."

"Yes Sir."

He continued, "We will not be returning to America for a while so advise the harbor master to make plans for relocation. Let's send him to Panama to ensure we avoid another situation."

Pleased that his agenda was understood Aiden Gina enjoyed dinner and retired to his office.

Outside in the employee parking lot a royal blue Lincoln parked in front of the harbormaster's shack. The harbormaster turned the surveillance systems off as Snitch exited in a beautiful hand-tailored suit with matching Italian stitched shoes. He walked onto the yacht and directly to the head of security and put his hand on his shoulder.

"Your loyalty will forever be held in my heart, the truck will take you and your men to the Irie Lock and a new Canadian vessel. Leave no remnants of his existence or ours on this vessel."

The security chief began to prepare his men immediately as Snitch made his way to Gina's office. He walked into the office of the yacht and stood in the shadow of the doorway. Gina smiled lighting his cigar as he sat behind his desk, "You are a very impressive man. Scary as hell, I must admit but you're efficient in the things that you do. The masterpiece you have helped me paint is almost complete and worth every dime. There's a place for a man like you in my organization I just need you to remove one more piece from the table."

Snitch stepped into the room allowing the light to show his face to Aiden for the first time. He asked, "Your organization?"

Gina took a hard gulp of his martini to center himself and stood up, he stepped to Snitch, "I know those eyes."

"If you know these eyes then you know that everyone involved in my father's betrayal must have their disloyalty accounted for."

"Son, I said your tactics are scary but you don't scare me." Gina boasted, "I'm the kingpin now. I am grateful for the work that you've done but the Fregoso organization is now the Gina organization. If you came here to do something other than accept this contract for this worthless excuse of a man, you're in for a world of hurt. You kill me the world will hunt you down like an animal."

Snitch reach to the back of Gina's head grabbing the base of his neck to pull him intimately close and whispered, "My father spent a lifetime perfecting his chess game and he taught me that players willing to sacrifice their pieces in the name of victory are blind to inadvertent attacks. You would be king of your new organization if you had killed the king, but you didn't. My father died peacefully in his sleep long before I allowed you to believe you were now El Hefe."

Unable to articulate a syllable, Gina's eyes could not break their stare and his sense of self-preservation abandoned him with his newfound truth. Snitch gripped Gina's lower jaw placing the stunned man in a life-threatening vice grip, "Francisco Fregoso is and will ALWAYS be head of the Fregoso family. All that your arrogance accomplished was to invite the reaper to your doorstep."

Five of the seven bones in Gina's clavicle snapped-making him collapse violently destroying his vital nervous system connections as Snitch delivered the concluding jolt to whom was once his father's most trusted partnership. He watched the life fade from the guilt-stricken man's face as his body fell to the floor. Snitch reached inside of his inner jacket pocket and pulled out a passport and cellphone, he placed Aiden Gina's passport on the dead man's chest and sent a text from the phone and placed it on top of the passport.

Chapter 26

Directors Murphy and Arsenault sat in Jason Murphy's office. Director Arsenault stood up from his chair to look out of the window, "Jason, if Jeffries types that number in and it's him we are going to have to assume that both the FBI and CIA could be compromised."

Director Murphy stood up from his desk to stand beside Director Arsenault, "I know Paul. We need to make sure that when it happens a full security breach protocol is enacted on everything in his access." He put his hand on Paul's shoulder.

Paul walked back to his laptop, "Jason I need you to hear the call from Colorado."

Director Murphy looked at him puzzled, "What call?"

"The embassy call that stopped us from touching Frank. It's the call that only a Director level member of one of our agencies could have allowed to happen and now we know who."

He pushed play and they heard a familiar voice,

"Chief Kase, how may I help you?"

"Roughly twenty-seven minutes ago you accepted Frank Fregoso as a guest at your CIA facility under the obscure yet sworn testimony of a former syndicate arsonist. One Marisa Dubai."

"Who is this?"

"I'm calling from the Portugal embassy and I would like to advise you that we will make no inquiry into the release of Mr. Fregoso at this moment. We will however schedule a call at this time every day with Mr. Fregoso. I'm sure the CIA plans to volunteer their full services in ensuring that Mr. Fregoso's accommodations on Winchester Blvd are suitable for the duration of his stay. Correct?"

"Sir if you are calling from an embassy, please understand that you have reached a city facility and you would need to call the American embassy for any diplomatic inquiries."

"No sir. According to the Secret Service under section: 1534-H the embassy of the detainee's country of origin is allowed all requests. I assure you after you run your call procedure you will find my petition quite reasonable. Have a wonderful day CIA Section Chief Kase Richardson."

Paul looked at the battle warn director looking down at his palm and Director Murphy stated, "I guess it's time to get this started."

"See you in a couple of minutes Jason."

Director Murphy walked down the hallway and tapped lightly on Samuel's open office door, "Hey Samuel, I need you in my office- just give me three minutes, need coffee."

"Yes Sir." Samuel looked up from his laptop to acknowledge Director Murphy.

Murphy walked onto the main floor to talk to Sr agent Goodson then returned to his office. Samuel stood at Murphy's desk with the head of the CIA.

"How's it going with that number Samuel?"

Samuel looked at Paul booting up his laptop, "Jason o be honest, I've ran those damn digits through every database we have and the only thing I uncovered was a serial number off a candy bar in New Zealand."

"Let me give you a database you haven't searched." Director Arsenault turned his laptop to Samuel, "Think of it as a family tree search."

"The CIA has a family archive?" Samuel looked at Murphy.

"Samuel type in the number."

Samuel typed in the number and three men stood silent for a moment acknowledging what they all suspected.

"The search result has already triggered a response team and your team is standing by Samuel." Murphy continued. "You should probably go talk to John."

Samuel barged into John Tanner's office and sat down in front of the slightly offended Deputy Director.

"Hey John. I've been racking my brain for weeks now asking myself why? Why is the last thing a dying man would do is text himself? Why would Gina send himself a number that meant nothing? Any clue John?"

Samuel held his hand up stopping Deputy Director Tanner's response, "It turns out CIA agents get special numbers engraved into their service plaques, you can imagine my distress when I discovered that Aiden Gina texted himself your CIA service plaque number."

Tanner leaned back in his chair calmly, "My fucking plaque number? I don't even know that damned number- that clever son-of-a-bitch. Samuel before you were a member of the FBI, I was doing what it took to ensure your missions were successful as a soldier, understand that. I got a call from Aiden Gina a few years ago and he said that he was watching an old Congress reel of the US putting away hundreds of people, Americans and foreigners alike under the Rico act. Extraditing the world in the name of American justice. He went on to inform me that he was getting older and needed to secure his retirement. He said if he walked into The White House and said he wanted to confess his sins, that one of our many agencies would ensure that he lived the rest of his life like a king but there would have been a fallout from his testimony on American soil. The impact would shatter American leadership and I'm not sure the citizens of the United States of America could handle that kind of true reality. He proposed a deal- it was simple, Frank was 89 years old and dying and our military demands required our tech sources be protected. Only the head of the Fregoso organization could guarantee that protection so we bet on the horse that could finish the race. Regardless of what you think of me you will soon understand this game is not black and white. We don't get to pick that all the bad guys leave and the good guys stay. It's a nasty rotation Samuel and you do what you believe is the best. Every decision I make, I make as a Patriot to provide."

"If you say save the country Tanner I will jump over this desk and you will never see a courtroom." Samuel seethed.

"Do you know how naive you are at this moment?" Tanner laughed.

Directors Murphy and Arsenault stepped into the office and Director Murphy spoke up, "John, there are a lot of words that I have for you but most important is that you are no longer a standing member of any government organization."

"Am I under arrest Samuel?" Tanner stood up.

"No John. We're just going to take everything that belongs to Uncle Sam away from you and you will go home your battle will be with your lawyers."

Samuel looked at Paul as he grabbed John by the arm and escorted him out of the office with Samuel's team. Murphy looked at Samuel closing John Tanner's door, "Go ahead Samuel."

"It can't be like this. We can't just allow this to be the truth about the system in place to protect America from people like Tanner. I looked up to that man and he's right! He helped my whole damned squad in Baghdad. He can't just be this greedy, power hungry bastard willing to sacrifice his justice for political gain."

Jason took a moment to allow Samuel's chest to stop heaving and responded,

"Samuel justice is not bad nor good. Each event we face we must choose how we want to navigate. As men who stand up for something other than ourselves we face an uphill battle against men who obey their ego. The FBI will take this black eye Samuel but only if we allow ourselves to heal. I cannot tell you what part of John was good or bad, but I will tell you that John Tanner will be used as a living example to us all, that we need to hold the line- for each other and our sister agencies. We need to ensure that we are moving forward Samuel lost is not a bad place for a leader to be as he evaluates a new landscape, but his team needs to feel confident in what they have accomplished. We're going to become better because of this but right now we need to focus on your team and closing this case."

Charles escorted John Tanner to his car and as the men got to the door of Tanner's AMG, Charles stated, "This is fucking treason Tanner and you are being allowed to smile your ass out of here to go hide under political red tape."

Tanner remained stoic patiently waiting for Charles to allow him access to his vehicle. Charles leaned towards John's ear and whispered, "If it were up to me would put you in Frank's old cell and just wait. Enjoy your freedom you fucking coward."

***

That evening Samuel left the office driving downtown and walked around lost in the emotional hurricane that had become his existence. Unable to find peace he found a bar and ordered an old fashioned. The bartender brought his drink and Samuel raised the glass looking in displeasure. "Sir, did I not make your drink correctly?" the bartender asked.

Samuel forced a smiled as he put the drink down to grab his wallet, "No the drink is perfect it's just not the old fashion I need."

He hurried home. Samuel sat on the side of his bed and dialed. Her voice immediately put his mind into a calm place as he heard her say.

"Samuel are you okay? It's late love, what's wrong?"

He responded softly, "Gabbi I'm so sorry to wake you but I couldn't find our cliff alone. I'm lost in my own head and I don't know who or what to trust. All I want to do is tell you everything and here you tell me it's ok- but I can't tell you anything and I can't trust my own belief system."

"Samuel if your mind is confused it's because your foundation has been made unstable. I promise you my love the man that you are can stand confidently on your own foundation. Your beliefs are molded by what you hope to be truth and when that truth is challenged we tend to believe we are going crazy. Your mind is fine but you will need to rebuild your own foundation based on the facts your heart know to be true. I promise you once your precious heart is at ease your mind will find its way home."

Chapter 26

It had been two months since John Tanner's inditement and the president was having trouble securing what was once a very supportive state. Chicago was John's hometown and they believed him as he pointed to Washington for the blame in his accusations. The last two weeks on the campaign trail through Illinois found the President tired and frustrated from having to defend the administration from rumors of a trader. Tom's final stop was the "Windy City" and it held nothing back as they blew their steadfast opinions directly against the president's reelection campaign.

The President sat down in his hotel suite exhausted. The press had been hard on the administration since Tanner's inditement and his hands held his aching brain steady as his fingers massaged his eyes. He stretched gently noticing the open blinds and the beautiful Chicago skyline as his heart began to pound violently and his eyes focused on the reflection of the red dot sitting steady on his forehead. He heard a voice from inside the room, "Please stay calm Mr. President, your cry for help would only cause your death and the death of every man that enters through that door. Tom my name is Ontario Fregoso the 17th, Frank was my brother and I loved him very much. Aiden Gina's last act of decency was to make arrangements for John Tanner. Your act of decency will be to provide a safe environment to complete that task. You will do this quietly and with clarity. It's quite simple really, very calmly repeat it to the window until you see the light disappear."

"Has this all been about vengeance? You've done all this to honor your brother?"

"Tom I've done none of this." Ontario looking straight-faced, "This has not been my doing. This is an orchestration of the consequences of disloyalty."

"Are you going kill me?"

Ontario stood up and walked directly behind him, "The only reason you would die today, Mr. President is if you fail to remember your country's hiding places."

"Are you the new head of the Fregoso organization?"

"Tom, this is a young man's game. The Fregoso organization died with Frank. I've seen 94 years on this Earth and it wasn't until I was an old man that I was able to see that enjoying my family *was* the goal. Now enough questions Mr. President, his patients is not the same as mine."

Tom jumped when Ontario patted his shoulder and began to mouth instructions as a member of the NSA escorted Ontario to his car avoiding the secret service security protocol.

Chapter 27

Samuel walked away from a pile of folders on his desk and into Director Murphy's office.

"Jason, sorry I'm late," He said unenthusiastically. "but this closing transition is taking a lot of time John had several open cases and Kevin is focusing the team to get prepared for today's fallout. John's going to try to walk away from this clean when he could be a man and face justice."

"Samuel, Tanner's pulled every lawyer trick in the book and he's just getting warmed up. He says he has names and it was him that requested a congressional hearing."

Samuel responded, "We're never going to see him again, once he goes in those doors he belongs to the CIA. That committee is just there to entertain his ego."

"I know." Agreed Murphy, "I'm just waiting on Paul to come back to the podium and say he's been formally charged- no further questions."

Samuel looked down at his bracelet,

"John belongs in GITMO. I don't believe he's a traitor but his ego has no regard for humanity."

Jason looked down, "Samuel when John checks into Guantanamo Bay this case is closed."

Samuel scoffed. "I'm going to catch him Jason and make him pay!"

"Pay for what Samuel? Not killing Frank? Removing the ugliest people with the most power from the top? Or maybe gift wrapping a liar like John Tanner and handing him to us."

"So you're becoming a fan of street Justice Jason?"

"No Samuel!" Murphy fired back. "I'm a fan of justice. Those men and how they handle business took care of themselves."

"Jason you and I both know Snitch is out there and you want me to sit here and do nothing because John Tanner is about to spill his guts?"

120

"That's exactly what I want you to do Samuel," Murphy confirmed. "our justice system is based on shreds of truth and proof, we have neither on Snitch. We have a phone call that never happened and a sniper round with no gun-we have zero evidence. The Secret Service already determined that the profile of Snitch could not have been one man but a very highly connected organization. An organization that has had its leadership stripped and left in a state of chaos and classified as dismantled."

"Jason what the fuck do you mean closed? You and I know goddamn well that he is real and he is the only conductor of this orchestra. He has composed a bloodbath of clearing all the enemies out of the way. Jason we can't close this case he's still out there." Samuel looked at Murphy.

"Samuel the FBI received all of the credit for eliminating the entire Fregoso organization and yet you and I both know the FBI had nothing to do with it. Right now the Secret Service has agreed that our investigation is closed and considering we have not one shred of evidence to prove their allegations false, all we can do is stand down deputy Director Jeffries. It's time to move on Samuel."

They turned the volume up on the big screen as John Tanner approached the podium surrounded by media.

"Former Deputy Director Tanner, can you tell us what you meant when you stated the American public deserves to know what's going on at the highest levels of politics? What are you about to tell the committee?"

John cleared his throat grabbing the world's attention, "I'm a good man-a Patriot. I served my country loyally as military personnel and under two government agencies. Anything I've done wrong I will confess here today, but all that I've done can be laid at the feet of our citizens and I ask for forgiveness. Those that are too arrogant to do the same will find out today that they too deserve to be punished. Behind those doors, the men and women that have the power to prosecute those oversized egos will find out who their real enemies are so they can be held accountable."

The former Deputy Director paused as the sniper's bullet entered his skull plowing through his cerebral cortex, exiting to the concrete stairs. The crowd dispersed in panic as security and police responded. Tanner's body fell backward thumping the steps and settling behind the podium.

Samuel stood looking at the TV with director Murphy as the team barged in.

Murphy addressed the team immediately, "We have to assume there is an active shooter in DC! Kevin mobilize now- Samuel and I will run code."

***

DC was cross-agency locked down according to the protocol and as the SUVs pulled onto the court lawn, CIA Director Arsenault walked out to greet the team. Murphy asked, "What happened Paul?"

"I don't know Jason, it was your AX50. The lockdown is complete with a full media blackout and we've got a 100% detained audience, every window secured and the scene has been cleared. Can your team run trajectory?"

Sarah spoke up as Kevin, Charles, and Cynthia began walking to the podium, "We're on it."

Director's Murphy and Arsenault walked with Samuel to the crime scene looking around at all the possible opportunity points.

"The court steps are surrounded by open groves then office buildings, the only known truth to any agency was that the round was fired from the seventh floor or higher." Murphy pointed out.

"John's preliminary report indicates that the projectile had to originate between ten and thirty- degrees from the podium and we have shooters and communication on every rooftop in the fire zone. Our interior intel confirms the round could not have been fired from any window vantage point. John twisted as the projectile entered and its trajectory was thrown off as it made impact on the stairs after exiting."

Assistant Director Goodson stepped up, "Thank you Paul. Let's recreate this. Charles you're about Tanner's height, take the podium. Sarah let's run trajectory reconnaissance from Charles."

The team began to mark off possible sniper locations as they meticulously communicated with each CIA rooftop sniper to confirm Charles's visibility. Cynthia looked at Charles standing at the podium as the last sniper made the check- unanimous that no building had the proper trajectory. Charles said, "If CIA was in every building that means he had no rooftop to shoot from and there's nothing higher."

Cynthia looked up at the Monument in the background and pointed,

"There's one thing higher!"

Director's Murphy and Arsenault looked at each other as their only cross agency alarm was triggered with Cynthia's observation and grabbed Samuel.

"We've got to go now AD Goodson!" Murphy shouted. "The CIA has this scene under control, I need you and your team to go fully armored to the Washington Monument and secure it now. Goodson, all the way to the top, I'll explain later."

"Yes sir." Kevin said quickly.

The team immediately responded as the three men drove the SUV's siren blaring through DC.

Murphy kept mumbling over and over to himself, "That lying son of a bitch was telling the truth."

"Murphy, what's going on?"

"Samuel when I confronted him about the cabin John said he would never break command unless I was outranked. I was so angry I discharged it as a lie to save his ass, but I had no proof. When Tanner gave his reason for siding with Gina he leaned on the Rico Act. Tanner took the law enforcement route to the FBI so the Rico Act would not affect him to the point of treason- it would require him to gain political power."

Samuel's eyes shifted between Murphy and Paul's, "That doesn't explain why we are speeding down Pennsylvania Avenue."

Director Arsenault spoke up, "Tom was once just a good lawyer recruited by the CIA after some extremely high profile wins and promoted his way to its highest position. Samuel only two people have the codes to gain access to the sniper's nest at the top of the Washington Monument and we are both in the vehicle with you. Only one other man alive has been a former director."

The horrifying truth sunk in as Samuel's phone began to ring. Samuel answered, "AD"- he paused and began again, "Deputy Director Jeffries."

Snitch spoke confidently, "Still getting used to the title huh Sam? It's okay it takes time. Sam you know there is no one that will be able to protect him when it's his time."

The line went dead.

Samuel yelled, "Hello! Hello? He's gone!"

"It's ok Samuel," Director Arsenault comforted, "Your line has an advanced tracking package- we will have him soon. What did he say?"

Samuel replied, "He said we can't protect him."

The three men made their way to the west wing and stood in front of the president. The Secret Service stood with them as Murphy began to speak, "Tom that shot came from a place only a few people in this room know exist. Just like the cabin in Tennessee and the medical offices in California."

The president stood up, "What are you asking Director Murphy?"

"Tom, how did you know Frank Fregoso was in California?" Director Murphy raised his eyebrow looking at the President.

"Jason I think you're forgetting the pecking order of things." He walked around his desk. "I would watch my tone- unless there's someone alive that would entertain those allegations?" He stopped giving Murphy a challenging look. "Since there is not Director Murphy, I would suggest you prepare your building for a Senate oversight committee. A much-needed review into the corruption that was ex-deputy director Tanner. I would also suggest the CIA figure out very quickly and very quietly just how national security was breached in broad daylight and find a way to make Americans feel safe again."

Samuel, fed up with the ego battle in the Oval Office spoke out, "No disrespect, Mr. President, but do you think our citizens will feel safe knowing that your life is in danger?"

"What the hell are you talking about Jeffries," President Tom Denning asked.

"He called me on the way here. Your name's on his list Tom and for the sake of self-preservation I suggest you cooperate with the FBI and CIA. Tell your Secret Service and The Senate committees that we are all on the same fucking side. Snitch said we can't protect you. Now, either you find a way to look past your arrogance and listen or you might find yourself like Tanner because for whatever reason this guy wants you in his crosshairs."

"The last time I checked ensuring that I stay out of all the crosshairs is the job of everyone in this damned office! Samuel if you have a killer calling you I suggest you do something about it." Tom fired back bouncing his gaze to all the men in the Oval Office. He grinned as he exhaled, "I'm not going to lose my re-election so you can chase a ghost. My sources have assured me that no one-man could have dismantled the Fregoso organization and no one-man could have pulled off what you claim Snitch is solely responsible for."

Samuel blurted, "You're going to lose because you are dead Tom. This guy called me from that office just behind that door." He pointed to a side door, "Advanced CIA tracing Mr. President so, if you feel safe then maybe you can tell me how Snitch used a phone in an office only Monica knew how to sneak into?"

Chapter 28

President Tom Denning set comfortably in CIA director Paul Arsenault's office. Tom crossed his arms on the director's desk, "Behind these doors our conversations don't exist, that being understood you and I both know Frank was dying. The Intel collected by all agencies confirmed that- he was pushing 90 and no one had indicated who his predecessor would be. The decision I made to protect this country's investments in the arms race was the only decision to make at that point in time. The Fregoso organization is not one man- its a conglomerate. A well oiled machine working for well over a decade with Frank on vacation. His illness made my decision necessary. On the record as president of the United States of America it is time for me to show the world we are still top of the food chain. No more hiding Director I won! How perfectly clear is that Paul?"

Director Arsenault sat back in his chair, "Tom it's crystal clear and as always Mr. President the CIA will stand by awaiting your direction, but Tom, you and I both know that it wasn't a corporate decision to stand against Frank Fregoso. If it would have been you would have called me to pick him up. This was an ego call Mr. President it has served you well but I don't share your opinion on the Fregoso family. We are not and never have been in competition with them, they just happen to be the best store in town."

Tom stood up pressing his lips together tightly stroking his chin, looking at Director Arsenault, "As former director of the CIA I'll tell you that this country's secrets are ugly but progress can be ugly director."

He Looked up at President Denning, "The CIA stands 100% behind the Commander in Chief, Sir. I apologize if my words made that questionable in any way."

Tom broke eye contact looking down at his shoes, "Very well and Paul, allow me to tell Jason in person before you pick up your phone. Have a good day Director Arsenault"

Tom left his Secret Service at the door and entered Murphy's office. "I hope you two are working on the normalization of our country."

Deputy Director Jeffries sat back in his chair, "What is normal to you Mr. President?"

Tom turned around to ensure none of his Secret Service were listening at the door and said boldly,

"Deputy Director Jeffries normal is not winning re-election by the grace of God-while hiding from the outside world. The FBI and CIA ran their scanners and frisked down every single one of my supporters. I had to run my campaign never once stepping outside. I looked like a fucking coward to my country because of a treasonous former FBI deputy-director who decided to cut a deal with the devil. I've done everything both of you lovely gentlemen have asked me to do and quite frankly I'm tired of it. The CIA and FBI need to understand that I am the President of the United States and I will be for the next four years. I will no longer hide under an umbrella of fear brought forth by a man we haven't heard from in more than six months. Yes I am still alive Samuel and yes, we did follow all your protocols Murph but this stops today. I will be addressing the American public in front of the entire world, here are all the details." He handed the men folders.

"I trust you gentlemen will continue to do your job so that I may continue to do mine." Murphy stood up holding the manila folder and The President continued,

"This isn't up for discussion Murphy. I'm the fucking boss- the leader of the free world."

He turned and walked out leaving the door open as the Secret Service looked in and slowly turned to escort the president to his vehicle.

As the president left the office Samuel proclaimed, "America deserves better."

Director Murphy sat down looking at the President's itinerary,

"Samuel America doesn't have a lot of men like you but right now the President does. Let's see what we are facing."

Director Murphy flipped through the intel, "On the steps of the National Archive Museum."

Samuel Dropped his head, "That is a nightmare to cover there are buildings everywhere. What the hell is he thinking?"

"Samuel every situation has a strategic plan this one is no different regardless of where we stand with whom we're protecting. Our job is to make sure we cover all bases. I'll get Paul on the huddle room speaker while you gather AD Goodson and his team."

***

They gathered as Directors' Murphy and Arsenault secured the huddle room line. Director Arsenault began, "Good afternoon team. I have Section Chief Kase on the line with me and I would like to give the mission overview to Deputy Director Jeffries and his team since you all are the experts on our sniper, what are we looking at?"

Samuel started, "We have a week-long event consisting of four days of formal dinners, culminated by the speech at the archives. There will be hundreds of windows and vantage points facing him- commercial and residential. I suggest we learn from Tanner's assassination and cover this like a traditional presidential speech but I want to own every supporter. We bring in full agency cooperation- CIA, FBI, DEA, DOD, and the Secret Service. We will be his crowd, we'll border the rooftops with snipers and an agent inside of every resident and business with a window view of the speech. Director Arsenault we will rely on CIA snipers with FBI spotters to ensure that every vantage point has our gun there. I want no compromised space."

Section Chief Kase broke in, "Jeffries I know we have the manpower and the know-how to pull that off but how do we stop the president from realizing his crowd is A.I.?"

Assistant Director Kevin Goodson answered, "We play to his ego. Our cameras and our media will be at the foot of the stairs, spotlights and flashes smothering that podium on a nationwide feed 10 seconds delayed at home and 15 offshore. When he's done Kase will lead the Secret Service directly to him and into the museum and during the applause and Cynthia, Sarah, and I will usher in actual supporters and the DEA can line the parade exit route with real constituents."

"That keeps everything in front of us." Samuel added. "Charles I want you with me and both Directors in the monument nest-no blind spots this time."

Director Murphy smiled, "Paul I'll split the calls with you, let's consult our brothers and sisters, we only have 3 months to pull this off. Let's get our bases covered and get ready for a speech we don't want to hear."

Chapter 29

The President stood at the interior doors of the National Archives Museum listening to hundreds of what he believed were his constituents cheer his name. All waiting to hear the words he had for the nation. He reached in his blazer pocket to answer his private phone and heard,

"You betrayed my father for political power Tom, and loyalty demands that everyone involved in the king's betrayal receive proper punishment. You broke your loyalty with a phone call to the FBI to celebrate your first term in office. As you look across that sea of supporters in front of your podium ask yourself, are all your agencies' snipers loyal to you? Or does their loyalty have a price? There are a lot of windows in front of you Mr. President, I'm looking forward to hearing your speech."

The phone went dead as the Vice President received the all clear from Kase and introduced the President to thunderous applause.

Samuel stood scanning the President's speech with Director's Murphy and Arsenault and with Charles at the sniper rifle. As the president made his way to the podium and began his speech in front of the museum Samuel's phone rang.

"Deputy Director Jeffries," he answered.

The voice said calmly, "Sam."

Samuel replied, "Francisco I know why you believe you are doing right by your father but you can't finish this game."

"Your vision has vastly improved but you still haven't focused your gaze high enough Sam."

Samuel checked the President and said, "For the first time Francisco I am. I respect the belief system that has brought us both to this point but you have to understand that system isn't always the best. Francisco the last man responsible for Frank's death will pay for his wrongdoings. One day he will be brought to justice but today he will not fall to your justice. I respect a son's loyalty to his father Francisco, it was that loyalty that allowed me to put 20,000 agents on the ground. I can confidently say if you're hiding in this crowd you work for me. It's not going to end the way you need it to end Francisco."

The two men paused as if to consider each other's chess move and Francisco Fregoso the 27th broke their silence, "Former Assistant Director Samuel Jeffries, now Deputy Director Samuel Jeffries my father was right about you, you are a good man and a great agent. I have confidence you will rise to greatness but you still need to adjust your sights."

Samuel looked down at the president and tapped Charles on the shoulder. Charles viewed the area and confirmed with both Directors that it was all clear. Returning to his call Samuel said confidently, "No. I think."

He paused as the phone hung up and the president dropped to the ground. Not a shot was fired as the entire world stood mystified at the broadcast interruption message floating on their screens and smartphones.

***

The doors to the Oval Office opened slowly as Director's Jason Murphy of the FBI and Paul Arsenault of the CIA exited with the new President, Former Vice President Shanous, and members of the NSA. The president's advisers joined him as he walked away and Paul and Jason made their way to Samuel.

"What are we going to do Murphy?"

"We're going to give American's time to mourn their former president and forget about John Tanner's assassination. Samuel Tom died of a heart attack. It's a lot of stress running the free world and Tanner's betrayal was too much to carry while winning his re-election."

Samuel demanded, "The country deserves the truth."

Murphy smiled, "Which is why we're going with the medical examiner Samuel, this is not about towing the company line. It's about the only damn truth any of us have. Samuel only the Secret Service and Kase witnessed Tom's eyes bleeding and there was no trace of any foreign substance in his system so we have to go with what we can prove."

Samuel looked over Murphy's shoulder at the NSA huddled around the new President and forced a smile saying , "Our nation has an official cause of death and time to heel."

The three men stood in silence after five years of chasing a man neither could call friend nor enemy, finally looking high enough to see as the king sees and pledged their loyalty to a new era of justice, upon exiting the White House.

The end...

Don't miss out!

Visit the website below and you can sign up to receive emails whenever Orion Pharoah publishes a new book. There's no charge and no obligation.

https://books2read.com/r/B-A-NJYP-YUEXB

BOOKS 2 READ

Connecting independent readers to independent writers.

About the Author

My dyslexia made it easy to ignite my imagination and paint pictures with my words. I took the long road in learning the process of converting a great story into a great book, and will forever be humbly perfecting my craft.

I don't know if I'm a good writer but I know I'm a great storyteller and I have a unique vision that is expressed through my pen.

Read more at subconscious-chatter.com.

www.ingramcontent.com/pod-product-compliance
Lightning Source LLC
Chambersburg PA
CBHW021114130626
46554CB00002B/685